Three small bonfires burned brightly. Around them sat three figures, clothed in black with hoods up or bandannas tied around their heads.

In the center of the group was a woman.

They stopped their talking and leaped up to face Ruth.

Ruth remembered Alva's warning about the proctologists in search of a sacrificial victim. Her breath froze in her lungs. She could not make out their faces, only the glitter of narrowed eyes. They did not speak, but the biggest one took a step toward her.

"Uh," she began, her heart hammering with the force of a pneumatic drill. "Uh, well. I see you've found the beach."

The big man took another step and reached inside his vest.

"Uh, what a—a lovely night for a bonfire." Ruth's voice trembled.

Now all three figures began to move slowly in Ruth's direction.

"I'll just run and get some marshmallows!" she shrieked. Ruth scooped up Franklin and ran as fast as her middle-aged legs would carry her, reciting the Lord's Prayer all the way home.

Other mysteries by Dana Mentink

Trouble Up Finny's Nose

Fog Over Finny's Nose
A Finny's Nose Mystery

Dana Mentink

HEARTSONG
PRESENTS
MYSTERIES

To my little girls,
who are Mommy's biggest fans.

To my precious Lord,
for blessing me with two angels from heaven.

ISBN 978-1-59789-643-6

Scripture taken from the Holy Bible, New International Version®. NIV®. Copyright © 1973, 1978, 1984 by International Bible Society. Used by permission of Zondervan. All rights reserved.

All of the characters and events in this book are fictitious. Any resemblance to actual persons, living or dead, or to actual events is purely coincidental.

Cover design: Kirk DouPonce, DogEared Design
Cover illustration: Jody Williams

Our mission is to publish and distribute inspirational products offering exceptional value and biblical encouragement to the masses.

Printed in the U.S.A.

1

It's a toe." Ruth peered into the glass jar on the counter of the Plymouth Frock Dress Shop.

It was one day before the Finny Fog Festival kickoff, and Ruth found herself enduring another fitting for her costume.

Maude snorted. "How would a toe find its way to the middle of the golf course?"

"It's not a golf course—it's a putting green; and Alva says that's where he found it. He brought it here because he didn't know what else to do." Looking into the gargantuan mirror on the shop wall, Ruth added testily, "I know a toe when I see one."

"Hold still, Ruth, honey," said Flo from her position on the floor as she pinned some fluttery silver gauze to the back of Ruth's tunic.

Ruth grimaced. The silver tights were giving her a wedgie. Moreover, the putty gray disks that sandwiched her in between did nothing to complement her pasty complexion, wide shoulders, and robust bottom.

"Has anyone filed a report with the police?"

"You mean a missing-toe report?" Ruth peered at the gray bulb in the jar. The nail was longish and yellow, and a sprig of black hair sprouted just above the severed end.

"I presume that the toe belongs to someone who wasn't thrilled to lose it. Maybe there's a body around somewhere to match," Maude said. "That's what Alva has been blabbering about anyway, and for once I agree with the nutcase."

"Don't even kid about that." The village of Finny, California, might appear to be a tranquil beach getaway, but underneath, Ruth knew, all kinds of passions simmered in a vigorously bubbling broth. "Jack is on his way here. He said to leave it where it is and keep our hands off." The Jack in question was Jack Denny, Finny police detective.

"As if we would take the disgusting thing out of the jar." Maude sniffed. She rubbed the mole on her temple thoughtfully. "I can't believe Alva brought it here anyway. What in the world gets into him?"

Maude's four-foot-eight frame stood ramrod straight, her vertebrae as steely as her constitution. Even her hair was determined, defiantly maintaining its black color in the face of five decades of living. Ruth was again amazed that someone so unyielding had been a contortionist for the circus. Ruth had actually seen photos of the mighty Maude Stone neatly folded in half and stuffed into a vegetable crate.

Florence Hodges rose from her kneeling position and rolled up her tape measure. "He said he thought a squirrel might eat it and whoever lost it would need to get an artificial toe. It was thoughtful, actually." She unfurled a pink Kleenex to wipe the patina of sweat that sparkled on her round face and dampened her red hair. The rest of Flo was round, too, and as pliable as a jelly doughnut.

"That man wouldn't know thoughtful if it ran him over," Maude huffed.

"Just because you have issues with Alva doesn't make him a bad person." Flo pointed to the toe. "Looks a bit rough. Could have used some moisturizer, I'd say. By the way, have you tried the new hydrating lotion at Puzan's? It really soothed my skin after I dug up my potatoes."

"I told you it was too early to dig them up," Maude said. "They're going to be bitter."

"Mr. Hodges seems to like them just fine." Flo calmly pulled her hiked-up pants back down over her meaty calves.

"Mr. Hodges would eat anything you put in front of him, including the tablecloth."

"That's because he loves me and appreciates my cooking," Flo said mildly. "And he's never eaten a tablecloth. Once he swallowed a pink birthday candle, but that was purely by mistake." She attempted to gently cram a circle of tinsel onto Ruth's flyaway hair.

Tearing her gaze from the orphaned toe and her ears from the arguing women, Ruth surveyed her appearance in the mirror again. "I look like a giant silver hubcap," she said.

The huge cardboard disks she wore on her front and rear were spray-painted silver and festooned with shiny swaths of metallic satin. Her legs were squeezed into silver tights. She continued to look at her reflection, convinced that a nearly forty-eight-year-old woman had no business being within spitting distance of spandex.

Maude paced like a nervous tiger around the front lobby of the dress shop. "Don't be ridiculous," she directed around a mouthful of pins. "You look exactly like a fog bank, doesn't she, Flo?"

Flo was the unflappable leader of the Finny Ladies Organization for Preparedness, which lent itself to the unfortunate acronym FLOP. She had long ago cultivated a poker face to deal with disasters that visited the seaside town of Finny from time to time. She assisted in crises of all kinds, including the death of Ruth's husband four years ago, and ironically, she'd made the cake for Ruth's wedding to Monk several months ago. She looked solemnly at Ruth in her shroud of silver and remarked, "Maybe we ought to revisit this mascot concept, Maude."

"I agree," Ruth piped in. She had begun to rethink the idea almost as soon as she had been roped into being the character mascot for the first ever Finny Fog Festival. Finny could not boast any luxury hotels or quaint shopping districts, but *fog* the town had in abundance. Maude was the publicity chairperson for the festival and a hard woman to refuse. She had planned a full three days of foggy fun and frolicking. "Why do we need a mascot anyway?"

Maude's bun bobbed indignantly. "Why? Because we need this festival to be a success, that's why. We need something to bring people to Finny. Something to make visitors forget that people have recently begun to get murdered here." Her voice bounced off the racks of hangers. For a tiny woman, she was gifted with the lungs of a longshoreman. "And now with this toe business, we need all the positive press we can get."

Ruth had to admit Maude had a point. The whole

mess two years ago had certainly not encouraged much tourist activity for the tiny town. Something about homicidal maniacs on the loose and the fact that Finny had nothing remotely resembling a mall kept people away. Visitors to the California coast seemed more inclined than ever to bypass Finny on their way to better-known stops, like neighboring Half Moon Bay.

"I think the Fog Festival will be enough of an attraction. People will come for the food and the crafts and music. They don't need a walking fog bank." Ruth heard a hint of desperation in her own voice.

"The kids will love it, getting their picture taken with Mrs. Fog. Speaking of pictures, have you taken those shots for the photo display posters?" Maude continued with the tenacity of an aggrieved pit bull. "You've just got to—"

A horrendous crash caused Maude to drop her pins on the shop floor. The three women ran out the front door to investigate.

They were met by a tangle of bicycle parts, human limbs, and little balls bouncing in multihued confusion in every direction. Delicate puffs of feathers floated lazily in the morning air.

"Alva! Are you all right?" Ruth raced to the fallen octogenarian, who lay upside down on top of a battered bike. Underneath the Alva layer was another human figure lying prone on the sidewalk.

"Yep. Right as rain." He clambered to his feet. "I was going faster than a greased pig when Martha flapped right out in front of me, crazy bird. I couldn't see, and I hit that guy. I dropped my bag of gum balls, too."

Alva Hernandez straightened slowly, cramming his fuzzy hat back over the equally fuzzy strands of white hair. After surveying the scene for a minute, he dropped to his knees and started scooping up the gum balls, shoving them in his pockets.

Ruth groaned. Most of her flock of crippled seabirds collected by her late veterinarian husband were content to stay in the backyard while she was away, but after one of the flock was maimed last year, Martha had become Ruth's shadow. Martha threw up such a squawk and a holler that Ruth had taken her along to the dress shop. The bird sat contentedly, sunning herself on a bench outside the shop. At least, that was where Ruth had left her, figuring a bird with a missing wing and a partial right foot could not get too terribly far.

Maude and Flo were already gingerly prodding the figure on the cement.

"Alva," Ruth said as she walked carefully between the skittering gum balls to join them, "why were you in such a hurry?"

The man lying on the ground began to grunt and mumble. He was egg shaped, bluntly round at the top, widening to a gentle oval in the middle where his black leather belt was cinched around his jeans. She was mesmerized by his head, completely bald and shining like the glistening flesh of an onion after the dry skin has been removed.

Maude assisted the man in rolling over and sitting up. The front of his head was every bit as dazzlingly white as the back. He might have been an albino except for the pale blueness of his eyes and a faint blush of color in his eyebrows. His glasses sat crookedly upon his nose.

"Wh–what happened?" he said, blinking furiously.

"We are so sorry," Flo spoke up. "It was an accident."

"Yes," Maude said, glaring at Alva. "Some people should not be allowed to operate moving vehicles. Especially *old* people."

A resident of Whist Street, Maude had earned her nickname of the Wicked Witch of Whist. She funneled her wrath to Alva, whom she accused of stomping on her primroses, and to the police, who refused to incarcerate him for the crime. Ruth had witnessed her leap onto the desk of a Finny police lieutenant, where she remained for an hour protesting Alva's mistreatment of her flowers.

"I don't think it was Alva's fault, exactly," Ruth said and then looked down at the stranger's gaze. "I'm awfully sorry. My bird walked in front of him and he swerved into you, I'm afraid."

He blinked translucent eyelashes again. His face was smooth and unlined, round and full like the rest of him. The man was much younger than his bald scalp first suggested.

"Can we help you up, Mr.—?" Flo asked.

Two more blinks. "Honeysill. Ed Honeysill." He offered his hands, and the three women grabbed onto his arms and hauled him to his feet.

"It's a pleasure to meet you," Maude said, pumping Ed's hand vigorously. "I am Maude Stone, chairperson of the Finny Fog Festival, and this is Flo Hodges and

Ruth Budge, my assistants."

Ruth felt the bit of discomfort that commonly arose at her continued use of her late husband's last name. It seemed disloyal, somehow, to Monk. They both agreed, however, that no one in Finny would ever get used to a new name for Ruth, and Monk's last name presented certain problems. Duluth. Ruth Duluth, they both agreed, sounded like some kind of carnival ride.

Ed nodded, still dazed.

"Are you sure you're all right?" Ruth asked.

"I think so, yes. I'm fine." He straightened his glasses and blinked before gesturing to Alva. "Is he okay?"

Maude eyed Alva with disgust. The old man's pockets were bulging with gum balls. "He's fine. Alva, you know those can't be sold in the store after you dumped them all over creation. They're contaminated."

"I know. Goin' to keep 'em. Shame to let 'em go to waste."

"You can't chew them," Maude continued ruthlessly. "You don't have any teeth."

Alva's grizzled eyebrows drew together obstinately. "Do so." He removed his upper bridge and plopped it on the bench. It sat on the wooden plank, grinning in ridiculous pink gumminess. "See?"

Ruth suddenly remembered her previous train of thought. "Oh, Alva. You were going to tell us why you were going in such a hurry."

"It's on account of the proctologists."

"The what?" Flo said.

"Them radical proctologists. Saw them up nose,

looking to cause trouble. They hate people. Probably searching for one to sacrifice. Maybe a mechanic or a UPS driver or something. Probably where that toe came from."

The three women stared at him.

"What in the blue blazes are you talking about?" Maude hissed.

"A bunch of proctologists. Weird people with lots of gear, heading up nose. One of 'em had a knife. I saw it plain as day." He popped a scuffed purple gum ball into his cheek.

"Proctologists?" Ruth repeated.

The shiny-headed man spoke up. "Er, I think he might be talking about ecologists. I did see a group of people I recognized this morning. They are some sort of ecological gang dedicated to the liberation of the earth or some such thing." He regarded the confused group before him. "They are pretty radical, I understand."

"Oh yeah," Alva said around the gum ball. "Maybe they did say ecologists. Anyway, I'm fixin' to get to the cops afore they off anyone around here."

Maude shook her head. "Pay no attention to him, Mr. Honeysill. He's an idiot, but a harmless one. What brings you to Finny? Did you come for the Fog Festival?"

"In a way. You're featuring some local produce at your festival, and I'm in fungus."

All three women looked at him blankly.

"I market edible fungus to restaurants along the coast. Mushrooms, truffles, and the like. I have a few things to check out here in Finny, one of which is the

Pistol Bang Mushroom Farm. I hear they have a booth at the festival."

Alva's head shot up. "That was my granddaddy's outfit," he lisped.

"Oh, really? Are you in the mushroom business?"

"Not anymore. Newspapers now."

"You publish a newspaper?" Ed looked impressed.

"Not publish, deliver." Alva put his teeth back in and mounted his bike. "Gotta go to the store and tell 'em about the gum ball mess before I file my report with the coppers."

"Don't you need to apologize to this gentleman?" Maude demanded.

"Sure. Sorry, Mr. Honeypot. See you around." Alva wobbled away.

Ruth, jumping into the pause that followed Alva's shaky departure, decided to try to make amends for the melee Martha had caused. "Actually, I know the woman who runs the business now. She bought it a few months ago. I could take you there, if you'd like."

"Really?" Ed's eyebrows moved up on his bare forehead like wiggly blond caterpillars. "How about this afternoon? I'm only here for the first weekend of the festival, so I'd like to cover as much ground as possible."

"Okay." She caught a glimpse of a feathery bottom scooting under the bench. "I'll meet you here, say around three? Will that work?"

He nodded. "Is it far?"

"A couple of miles. Straight up Finny's Nose." She bent over and plunged under the bench. The feathery bottom scooted out the other side. Upright again, she noticed that Ed's caterpillar eyebrows had crawled upward again in confusion.

"The big hill. We call it Finny's Nose," she explained.

"It's all part of the colorful history of our quaint little hamlet," Maude interjected. "Ruth is doing a historical booklet on the history of Finny, complete with pictures. She's our photographer, when she's not busy with her other career."

Ed nodded politely. "What business are you in, Mrs. Budge?"

"She's a vermiculturist," Flo said.

Ruth noted the blank look on his face. She would have been surprised to see any other kind of look. "A worm farmer. I operate Phillip's Worm Emporium."

He smiled. "A worm farmer? Now I've never heard of that one before. How do you plant worms?"

"No planting required, just lots of hard work."

"I imagine living on the coast like this generates a good business from fishermen types looking for their bucket of night crawlers."

"Night crawlers reproduce too slowly to do well in a commercial venture. My husband and I farm red worms."

"Incredible," Ed said. "What do you do with them?"

"Most are sold for bait-and-tackle purposes, but I also sell the castings to organic farms like Pistol Bang's, and a few florist shops. The smaller ones I sell to local pet shops. I even supply high schools for their composting program, if you can believe it."

She dove with as much grace as she could muster behind a ceramic pot full of rosemary. Her fingers grazed Martha's wing, but the bird wriggled out of her grasp.

"I'd better get checked in at the hotel," Ed said.

Florence executed a sneaky end-around maneuver and caught the unsuspecting Martha. The disgruntled bird flapped her pewter and white feathers. Flo dusted off the naughty gull before handing her back to Ruth.

"You would never pass an obedience class, you bad thing." The bird tucked her head under Ruth's chin and fell asleep. "Okay, Mr. Honeysill. Three o'clock it is." There was some hesitation in the man's expression. "Is there something else?"

"Er, I was just wondering."

"Yes?" she prodded.

"Why are you dressed like a hubcap?"

Ruth sighed. "It's a long story."

Ed was as blindingly luminous in the afternoon sun as he had been in the morning. The light shone off his bald head like the coronas that surrounded the saints in old religious paintings. It was startling to see such display of scalp on a man still in his thirties.

Standing with him, arms crossed, was a tall woman with skin the color of the crystallized top on a crème brûlée. Ruth could not decide if she was African American or perhaps of Indian descent. She wore a cropped yellow shirt and low-slung jeans. Ruth didn't think her own stomach could ever be that flat, short of extreme liposuction and an industrial iron.

"Hello, Mr. Honeysill. Did you get settled into the hotel okay?" It was not a luxury hotel by any stretch of the imagination, but on weekday mornings, the nearby Buns Up Bakery whipped up a batch of their delectable apple fritters and the hotel patrons were treated to an onslaught of delirium-producing fragrance. Other than that, an extra roll of toilet paper and a free copy of the *Finny Times* were about the only amenities.

"We're all checked in. Ruth, this is my wife, Candace. She decided to join me on this trip to spend some time on the beach. We live in Arizona, so beaches aren't easy to come by."

The woman smiled and pushed a fringe of long straight hair from her eyes with a French-tipped fingernail. "Pleased to meet you. Where is the beach, by the way? All I've seen so far is fog."

"It dissipates in the afternoon usually. The fog, I mean," Ruth said. "I'm afraid our beaches might not be what you're expecting. They're mostly gravel, and the water is only suited for the supremely committed." She had to admit gleaning a certain perverse amusement from the tourists who came to this tiny corner of California expecting to bask in sunshine but instead immediately dashing off to buy sweatshirts. "You have to go farther south to find tanning rays and sunny beaches."

Candace nodded. "I guess I should have checked my AAA manual before I packed my bathing suit."

Ed kissed Candace on the neck and pulled the

shirt up around her shoulders. "I'll make sure my next business trip puts us around Pismo Beach."

Ruth noticed a faint look of annoyance steal over the woman's face.

"Well, shouldn't we be getting to the top of this nose thing?" Candace asked.

As they walked, the sun gradually emerged until only faint whispers of fog remained. The slope was graveled and muddy in places. Wild mustard blanketed the hills between clusters of twisted oak and cedar trees. A sweet smell of new blossoms greeted them. Ruth paused occasionally to act as tour director.

"Frederick Finny settled here after his ship ran aground trying to deliver a load of bootleg Canadian liquor. He tried dumping the rum into the water to lighten the load, but that only resulted in drunken crabs."

They continued on until they reached a flat, grassy plateau buzzing with activity. On the perimeter of the area, people were constructing booths and tacking up signs. Farther away, a group of men wrestled what appeared to be a giant sleeping bag. One man fought with a green fabric mountain, while another tinkered with an enormous wicker basket.

Ruth saw Maude deep in conversation with a third man who stood away from the group. Her mouth fell open as she watched her friend finger her hair and giggle. Yes, it was definitely a girlish giggle, emanating from the mouth of the Wicked Witch of Whist.

Maude looked less than thrilled when she noticed the group of three approaching. Eyes narrowed, she asked, "What are you doing here?"

Ruth said sweetly, "Don't you remember? I'm giving Mr. Honeysill a tour of our wonderful hamlet. We're heading up nose. This is his wife, Candace. Candace, this is Maude Stone, chairwoman of our festival. Would you like to introduce us to your friend?"

The man standing next to Maude was, Ruth had to admit, very pleasing to the eye. He had close-cropped blond hair, wide shoulders, and muscled arms straining against the confines of his T-shirt. She thought he looked like Superman, only slightly less inflated.

"Hello. I'm Bing Mitchell. I'm the owner of this balloon company, Phineas Phogg Hot Air Adventures. I'm here to do a few demonstrations for your festival."

Ruth introduced her two traveling companions. Bing took Ed's hand and then his wife's. "I've had the pleasure of meeting Candace before." He gave her a warm smile.

Ruth thought for a moment that it was a shade too warm.

"Are you both here for the festival, too?" Bing asked.

Ed nodded. "Sure are. Just checking out the local fungus. You do look familiar to me. I think we saw you when we were up in Oregon. Isn't that right, hon?"

Candace nodded. "Yes. I got to watch him inflate the balloons while you were networking," she said.

Ruth noticed a tiny stroke of sarcasm in the woman's tone. "Is this where you launch the balloons and land them?"

Maude piped up. "Oh, that's not how it works.

It's practically impossible to land a balloon in the same spot it was launched from on account of the wind and all. Isn't that right, Bing?"

He smiled, dimpling. "It's largely improvisation and luck. We can generally land in the right vicinity. Don't worry, we won't take your visitors to Kansas or anything. We're just going to anchor the balloon and send it up so people can get a bird's-eye view of Finny and the ocean."

"Sounds like a popular attraction to me," Ruth said. "We're on our way to tour Pistol Bang's."

He laughed. "I just love this place. It's a slice of life, all right. I really need to shoot some video. It's a hobby of mine." He looked toward the open field where two men in Phineas Phogg T-shirts were starting the long process of inflating the balloons. "Well, I need to get back to work. It was a pleasure meeting you all, and seeing you again, Candace."

Ruth watched Maude follow Bing's departing form, a dreamy expression on her face. Then she realized that the Honeysills had continued meandering their way up nose. She left Maude to her ogling and hurried to catch up with the Honeysills, nearing them just in time to catch the hint of anger in their conversation.

"—just saying maybe there is a way to be in the black without threatening your high moral fiber." Candace snapped out the words like rubber bands.

"Quality and integrity—that's how to build a business, Candy; you know that," Ed said.

"Didn't you ever just do something without thinking of the morality or sensibility of it? Just do it because it feels right?"

He stopped and turned to face her. "As a matter of fact, yes. I married you. Just because I love you, and it feels right." He reached out a hand to her.

Ruth saw her fold her arms across her chest. She almost didn't catch her response.

"Maybe it doesn't feel right to me anymore," the young woman whispered.

Ruth cleared her throat as she caught up. "Well, that was interesting. I've never met a balloonist before. This fog festival is really opening up our world."

Candace nodded faintly, and they resumed their walk.

"How far up nose are we headed, Mrs. Budge?" Ed asked.

"Call me Ruth. It's just another mile or so, but it's an easy walk. I take the birds up here all the time because there's a pond where they can get their water fix."

"You have more than one bird?" he asked.

"Yes, currently I've got seven of the feathery monsters. One was delivered to me from the animal clinic just last week, minus a gangrenous leg and an eye that he lost tangling with a cat. Milton is doing well, but he's going to have to toughen up a bit to get anything to eat in my backyard."

Candace slowed to walk next to her. "Where did you come up with that name?"

"My first husband, Phillip, named all our birds after the presidents. I decided to carry on the family tradition."

"Ed told me that you have a business—Phillip's

Farm or something like that?" Candace said.

"Phillip's Worm Emporium. My husband, Monk, and I raise worms for commercial sale."

Candace looked at her as though she were speaking in another language.

Ruth felt the strange intermingled pride and sadness that came when she told people about the farm. The ridiculous name emerged from one of their running jokes. At the same time, she embraced the strength that began to grow when she dove into the silly idea and made it a profitable business. Phillip would be proud of her, and it felt good. She knew he also would be happy she had found a good man to share it with, an amazing man of tireless strength who rubbed her feet and knitted sweaters. She enjoyed, too, the knowledge that she and Monk were partners, each helping the other's business to succeed. Monk embraced his worm-tending duties as cheerfully as she did her work at his catering business.

"I hear you've got someone in the truffle business here," Ed said. "That's a specialty of mine."

"Hugh Lemmon. He's just starting a new venture." Ruth paused for a moment. "How does a truffle grow, anyway? I only know about mushrooms and worms."

"They live in symbiosis with the roots of specific trees. The truffle passes nutrients and water to the tree and in exchange absorbs sugars for itself. The rarity comes in because there are many fungi that can provide the same service to the tree, so they all compete for space in the root system." He scratched his shiny scalp. "The truffle fungus doesn't win out all that often."

"So it's a truffle-eat-truffle world out there?"

"If you're lucky. You can't really weed out competing fungus species, so the only two choices are trying to provide hospitable conditions for the truffle fungus to take hold, or finding them in the wild."

"That's where the pigs come in?"

Ed laughed. "Actually, dogs do better because they don't gobble up the prize."

They emerged from a copse of trees onto the driveway of the Pistol Bang Mushroom Farm. The first building to greet them was a stone structure, with two small panes of glass serving as windows and a thick wooden door. The shingles were covered with a veneer of grizzly moss. A mushroom-shaped mailbox stood on a post off to one side, flowering clematis vines doing their best to smother it.

"Dimple must be in the back. Let's go around and see." She led the way into a burgeoning garden area. An irregular stone pathway ambled hither and yon through a collection of flowering shrubs and spiky grass mounds. The newly emerged sun bathed the whole mélange in dazzling light.

"Oh, it's gorgeous," Candace said. She stooped to finger the lacy white hydrangeas twined over a rough pine bench.

"Dimple is an amazing gardener. She studied botany in college." Ruth was surprised to hear an almost maternal tone in her own words. "She took over the property two years ago and began a complete overhaul, starting with building the tunnel. It's quite an astonishing place, really. Those logs over there standing next to each other are oak, waiting to be inoculated."

The logs stood close together but not touching, like miniature sentries alongside the ten-foot-tall polytunnel. A delicious smell of sawdust and hot wax hung in the air as the threesome made their way to a small workshop on the far side of the garden.

Two heads were bent over the rough workbench, Dimple's long blond hair obscuring most of Hugh Lemmon's unruly black mop.

"Hello," Ruth called. "We're here for the tour."

Dimple and Hugh lifted their heads in unison.

"Greetings," Dimple said. "You must be Mr. Honeysill. I'm Dimple. We've spoken on the phone."

"Yes indeed, and this is my wife, Candace. Thank you for giving us the grand tour."

"You are very welcome. This is Hugh Lemmon, a dear friend of mine."

Hugh shook Ed's hand.

"I've heard about you," Ed said over the handshake. "You've got a line on some imported truffles. I'd love to see them. They're sort of a specialty of mine, and I'm always looking for new sources."

"That would be great." Hugh put down the metal gadgets cradled in his long fingers.

Candace spoke up. "What are you two working on in all this sawdust? I thought mushrooms grew in soil."

"Actually, my mushrooms grow on logs. Hugh is helping me with the inoculator." Dimple held up a metal contraption that looked like the leftover parts from a bicycle overhaul.

"Amazing." Ed's eyes shone with excitement.

"Yes. Hugh can do anything related to plants. Do you know he almost produced a blue geranium for his senior high project?"

Candace blinked. "Is that hard to do?"

"Have you ever seen a blue geranium?" Hugh wiped sawdust off of his long neck.

"Uh, no. Come to think of it, I never have."

"Well, Hugh almost did it," Dimple continued.

"What happened?"

"Cutworms," Hugh said shortly.

"What a bummer," Ed said. He picked up the inoculator from the table. "This is excellent, a real work of genius."

"We use it to drill holes into the log and impregnate the wood with mycelium. Then we cap it with hot wax," Dimple said.

Ruth struggled through her winding corridors of memory to recall what exactly mycelium was. Candace came to her rescue. "What's mycelium?"

"Mycelium? Don't you remember, honey?" Ed regarded her with surprise. "It's the mass of microscopic threads, the body, if you will, of the mushroom."

Candace raised her delicate eyebrows. "Now how could I have forgotten that?"

"Most edible fungi are saprophytic." He looked up and noted his wife's narrowed eyes. "Er, they get their nutrients from decaying matter." He fingered the inoculator gently and examined it from all angles. "You know, this is really something. Where did you come up with it?"

Dimple smiled, patting Hugh on the shoulder. "It's his design. He is a whiz at anything mechanical."

A blush crept over the young man's face.

It was not unusual to find Hugh at Pistol Bang's, though his efforts were purely voluntary. Ruth had not noticed before the level of intimacy between Dimple and the young man. Well, why couldn't there be? They were the same age, more or less, and what were the odds of finding a partner with a common passion for fungus?

"I learned a few things to help out my dad. He can grow anything green, but when it comes to machines, he can't figure out how to plug in a toaster." He wiped the sawdust off of his T-shirt. "I'd better be going. It was nice to meet you folks."

Ed called out to his rapidly vanishing back, "Hey, don't forget, I'd like to see your truffles."

Hugh did not turn around as he strode away down the garden path.

"He is very shy, Mr. Honeysill. I'm sure he'd love to show you his truffles," Dimple said.

"No problem. How about you show me some of your operation here and maybe we can talk about some sort of mutually beneficial arrangement?"

She gracefully shook the sawdust from the folds of her skirt and led them to the door. "Let's begin in the polytunnel."

Ruth was often struck by a strangely surreal feeling when she entered the polytunnel, like Dorothy landing in the middle of Munchkin country. It was dark and warm inside, the air moist and smelling of verdant forest. She could swear that in the total silence of the tunnel, you could hear the mushrooms multiplying, stealthily adding followers to their fleshy minions.

"Wow," Candace said. She craned her neck upward to see the top of the neatly stacked log towers, all bristling with tiny soft buttons, like millions of infant fingertips. "How many different types of mushrooms do you grow?"

"Just two. Oyster and shiitake. I have the greatest affinity for these two varieties. We understand each other," she answered dreamily.

Candace shot Ruth a questioning look. Ruth whispered in her ear, "She has an unusually close relationship with her plants."

"Incredible specimens," Ed said, poking his round head near the closest log. "So you age the logs outside after you inoculate them, close together but not touching to prevent any foreign mold from taking up residence, I would guess?"

Dimple nodded. "Yes. The mycelia colonize the wood for about two years. Then we shock the colonies by submerging the logs in cold water."

"Shock them?" Candace said.

"It is really very necessary, and not at all unpleasant as it would be to us. In the trials of today are written the fruits of tomorrow."

Ruth laughed, watching Candace try to decide if she had heard Dimple Dent right.

"They begin to pin shortly afterward." She glanced

at Candace. "That means sprout, and in about seven days they are just about mature."

Ruth marveled anew at the silky caps of the plump shiitake and the fragile splayed fans of oyster mushrooms. It struck her as magic, growing edible treasure in near darkness. "How many crops can you get out of one log?"

"I am not positive, as this is a new venture for me. These are on their fourth pinning, and I think they have one more burst in them before they decompose."

She expected to hear another wisdom-of-the-ages comment, but Dimple's mental train was derailed by Candace.

"Thanks for the tour. I'm going to admire the garden a little more if you don't mind."

Leaving Ed and Dimple to talk fungal facts, Ruth followed her out.

Both women stood blinking in the sunlight, appreciating the cool breeze on their faces.

"She's an original, isn't she?" Candace said, gesturing to the polytunnel.

"Dimple? Yes indeed, she's one of a kind."

"Is she a local girl?"

"Yes. Her father was a pumpkin farmer in Finny for years before he sold his land to developers."

"What about her mother?"

She hesitated, not wanting to betray anything too personal. "She left when Dimple was a girl. Her father raised her." *More like maintained than raised,* she added to herself.

"Oh. That's too bad. Maybe that kind of explains

her, er, originality. Does she ever see her mother?"

"Not since she left Finny twenty years ago." Ruth had to admit that when Dimple asked Ruth to assume the role of grandma to Dimple's daughter, Cootchie, a lot of maternal feelings grew for Dimple, as well. Ruth knew she couldn't fill the hole Dimple's mother had left, but she liked to think she made an adequate stab as substitute mom. A lizard scuttled over the walkway under a clump of yellow lupine. She noticed a slightly bored expression on Candace's face. "Are you enjoying your stay here?"

Candace twisted her long black hair into a rope and coiled it on top of her head, letting the breeze caress her neck. "I guess. To be honest, I'm a city girl. I'm from Miami, so this place is a tad slow for me." She sighed, letting the hair fall around her face. "I think this life is a tad slow for me."

"Do you travel with Ed often?"

"As little as possible. I can't think of anything more boring than visiting mushroom growers and trucking companies all day. Sometimes I come if it's a slow time at the office."

"What do you do?"

"I work for a real estate company," she said, and a spark kindled in her brown eyes. "I'm a receptionist now, but I'm working on getting my license. The man I work for specializes in finding getaways for celebrities. Private places where they have all the luxuries but away from the paparazzi and all that. He's got some really big clients." She rattled off a couple of names.

Ruth tried to cover her blank stare with an interested nod.

"You've never heard of any of them, have you?" Candace laughed ruefully. "I'm not surprised. It seems like this entire stretch of coast is stuck in some kind of time warp."

"Not true. We have running water and the Internet."

"Oh, I'm sorry. That probably sounded condescending. I really enjoy the coast; I guess I just need a faster pace."

And a faster husband? "If you don't mind my asking, how did you and your husband meet?" Ruth found one of the benefits to escaping a murderer a while back was that the experience seemed to remove some of her timidity. She didn't feel the need to restrain her nosy parker tendencies as much since the trauma.

"My father introduced us—can you believe it?" She rolled her eyes. "Mom died when I was eleven, and Daddy believed in the shelter-in-place method of child rearing. He sent me to private schools and kept me away from pretty near anyone except a few family friends until I went off to college."

She bent to pluck a mint leaf. "I went a little crazy with all the freedom. I guess it scared Daddy, because he cut off my tuition and brought me home. I am sure he considered finding me a nice room at the top of a lighthouse on some remote rocky island." She laughed. "Anyway, one of his dear old chums had a son—a nice, responsible sort, good provider, honest, true, a solid fellow. That's Ed. He seemed like a match made in heaven. To Daddy, anyway."

She dropped the leaf and brushed off her hands.

"I'm not being fair. Ed is a good man, and he loves me very much. I should remind myself of that more often."

Ruth saw the wistfulness in the young woman's eyes, and she wondered if Ed ever saw it there.

The tunnel door opened, and Dimple popped out holding a double handful of mocha-colored mushrooms. "Ruth, would you mind cooking these up for us so Ed and Candace can have a taste?" She glanced at her guests. "Ruth is the best chef in Finny. She cooks lunch for us at least once a week if we're lucky."

"Thanks for the compliment," Ruth said, taking the velvety bundle. "I'll be right back." She heard Ed asking Dimple for Hugh's address as she headed for the kitchenette in the back of the office building.

As she heated the olive oil and sliced the mushrooms, she thought about what an unlikely pair Candace and Ed were. She was lovely, hip, and craved a fast lifestyle. He seemed more at home with fungus than females. As the oil reached the sizzling point, she slid in the chunks of shiitake and minced garlic. In went a hefty tablespoon of butter, and the mouthwatering aroma soon drove thoughts of the Honeysills out of her mind. She couldn't resist taking a taste as she slid them onto paper plates and put the plates on a tray. Heaven. The mushrooms were meaty with a delectable smoky flavor.

Tray in hand, she marched back out to the poly-tunnel just as Ed and Dimple emerged, stepping from darkness to day. Candace settled onto a bench, and they joined her.

Dimple's smile vanished as she looked over Ruth's shoulder, and a bewildered look crossed her face. Ruth turned. There stood a well-manicured woman with perfectly coiffed hair.

"Everyone," Dimple said with a quiver in her voice, "this is Meg Sooner. She's my mother."

2

At the stroke of seven o'clock, both halves of the Finny marching band stepped off to begin the Fog Festival parade with a rousing march. However, due to a series of miscommunications and the thick blanket of fog, the brass and percussion sections started at the Save Mart, marching in a southern direction. At the other end of town, the drum major led the wind instruments and flag bearers northward from the town square after he tired of waiting for the missing brass and percussionists. The musical hordes met up at the Buns Up Bakery, where half the group about-faced to resume a more unified advance down Main Street.

Ruth and Cootchie sat in lawn chairs that Ruth had parked on the sidewalk just after sunup. Early birds get the best parade seating. Actually, she awoke well before the birds with a vague sense of unease. She tossed and turned for some time before medicating her anxiety with strong coffee and a fat cinnamon roll. Even after the cholesterol slam, she couldn't shake the strange unsettled feeling as she kissed her sleeping husband and headed out.

The source of her unease didn't hit her until she saw the fire engine rumbling down the street behind Lou Fennerman's Cub Scout troop. The strobing lights, the plaintive wail of the siren. Today was Friday, March second, the five-year anniversary of Phillip's death.

At first she had counted the loss in weeks and

months. She remembered past springs with a vague sense that she was a different person with each passing year. After Phillip died, she felt as if she were aging in dog years, growing exponentially older with every change of the calendar. She was a stranger even to herself, drowning in a profound grief. Until God threw her a flotation device.

It came in the form of a wafty woman named Dimple Dent. Somehow Ruth had managed to keep everyone else out with polite refusals and business. Jack Denny found his way in briefly, the night he asked for her help finding the dog that was the only link to his bereaved son. But no one else. No one until Dimple fell into her life.

Imagine a bizarre, fluttery woman asking a stranger to help raise her child.

Imagine a forty-six-year-old stranger saying yes.

And then came Monk, another answer to a prayer she didn't even know she'd prayed. Perhaps it was odd to house feelings of loss for a dead husband and love for a new one at the same time, but life was full of bittersweets. It had taken her many decades to learn that.

Now that Dimple's mother was back, she wondered if it was time for more bitter. The woman had appeared out of nowhere to upset the precarious balance of her life. Ruth shook the thought away. Now was not the time for melodramatics.

The copper-haired Cootchie squealed when she saw her mother and flapped her little hand in a greeting. Dimple carried a tray laden with glistening white mushrooms of every size and shape and sported a felt fedora with PISTOL BANG MUSHROOM FARM on the brim. She handed the parade goers samples of mushrooms in white paper cups. Most of the recipients gazed suspiciously at the tidbits.

Ruth laughed as Dimple kissed Cootchie and handed them both cups of satiny oyster mushrooms before continuing on her way. Only Dimple would think of passing out mushrooms like party favors. She had even gone so far as to suggest that Ruth pass around pouches of worms to advertise Phillip's Worm Emporium.

Ruth had politely declined.

"Bye-bye, Mommy!" Cootchie shouted.

Dimple blew her another kiss.

It was a short parade. The fire engine followed the Cub Scouts. The Daisy troop trailed behind the engine. Interspersed here and there were some locals on horseback and representatives from FLOP dressed in matching yellow slickers. Ruth would have to inquire about the significance of the rain gear. It seemed to her more appropriate for monsoon season than a fog celebration.

The pageant ended with towering librarian Ellen Foots leading a small brigade of tiny tots dressed as puffy gray clouds. Most of them carried a book in their chilled hands, and two carried a banner proclaiming "READING IS FOR EVERYONE!"

Ellen peered out from underneath her wild maelstrom of dark hair and fixed her glance on Ruth. "You'd better get up nose. You're supposed to be changed and ready for photos in thirty minutes." She marched on by. The young children struggled to keep up.

"Okay, Cootchie. Looks like Nana's not going to get out of this. Let's find your mommy so I can keep my appointment with humiliation."

Before they left, she turned and looked down the street at the departing parade. The thick blanket of fog swallowed up the sparkling costumes and cheerfully obnoxious music, sucking them into a clammy void. It was odd how the fog could absorb life, surround it and smother it as though it had never existed.

How strange that she had never noticed it before.

Fifteen minutes later, Ruth tugged vigorously at the silver tights riding up into uncharted territory. She waddled her way to the open field where most of the festival activities were grouped. She stopped for a minute to watch the Coastal Comet Acrobats juggle fruits from their perches on the shoulders of the less fortunate Comets. A voice of doom cut through the hubbub.

"Ruth, it's about time." Maude still wore her yellow slicker and rain hat. She looked like a homicidal Gorton's Fisherman. "I've got a line of kids here waiting to have their picture taken with Mrs. Fog." They had decided after several pointed comments from informal focus groups, notably the children enrolled at library story time, that Ruth would not pass for a Mr. Fog.

"I'm here, with my best cheesy smile," she said, waving gamely to the children.

"Where's your hat?" Maude demanded, stabbing a short finger at the top of Ruth's head.

"If you mean that silver tinsel stuff, I can't wear it because it tangles up in my hair." She felt she had presented her case very well.

Apparently there was no room for a soldier's opinion in this woman's army. "Fortunately," Maude said firmly, "I brought some extra. That first trailer over there is the festival headquarters. Go get some tinsel and I'll put it on you. Hurry."

Thinking how nice it would be to throw a bucket of water on the Wicked Witch of Whist, Ruth trudged over to the long rows of trailers parked on the periphery of the field.

She yanked open the door and shoved her disks inside. It took a minute for her eyes to adjust to the dimness. The small trailer was crowded on one side with a full bed and on the other with a tiny sink and microwave. Several empty bottles of Perrier were lined up neatly on the top of the microwave.

"Well, I guess the festival staff have been enjoying themselves," she murmured grumpily.

As she scanned the room looking for anything tinsel-like, she noticed a man's athletic shoes standing neatly in the bottom of an open closet. They were the expensive kind, with cushions of air in the transparent heels and no visible laces.

"Who in the world would be wearing those?" She just managed to finish the sentence when she heard voices outside the door. They didn't sound like Maude or Flo or Ellen or any of the other Finny Fog Festival soldiers.

"Oh!" Her hands flew to her mouth as it dawned on her that she was in the wrong trailer. In a moment of panic, she squeezed herself into the closet with the athletic shoes and pulled the door closed. A conversation floated through the gap, voices muffled but slightly familiar

"This is wrong, Bing. I shouldn't be here." The woman's voice was deep and trembling.

"Just relax, hon."

Ruth heard the sound of liquid pouring.

"Here," the man said above the clinking of glasses. "We both know why you came."

"We can't see each other anymore," the woman said quietly.

Ruth felt her calves cramp up, courtesy of her bent-over position. She tried to figure out where she'd heard the female voice before.

"How am I going to get out of this mess?"

From Ruth's closet vantage point, she could see only the sandaled foot of a woman with shell pink toenails. A still-functioning lobe of her brain registered that the sandals were quite lovely, turquoise leather with tiny silver and black beads threaded onto the slender straps.

The voices continued to escalate. *This is not my business,* Ruth thought to herself. Normally she didn't mind eavesdropping, but doing so from someone else's closet was unforgivable. She stuck her fingers in her ears and tried to recite the Girl Scout pledge in her head.

On my honor, she thought frantically, *I will try—*

"We can't do this," the woman's voice shrilled.

To serve God—

The volume got more intense until it eclipsed the pledge altogether.

My country and mankind—

"Why can't you take no for an answer?" The shell pink toes stamped the floor.

—And to live by the Girl Scout law, she thought as loudly as she could.

Just then the door slammed.

As she attempted to silently stretch out her leg muscles, she could see a sliver of the window next to the front door. The top of a woman's head disappeared down the front steps.

"Women," the man muttered.

The door slammed again, leaving her in silence.

After an eternity, Ruth extricated herself from the closet. Her knees were shaking, and she made her way from the trailer area as quickly as her voluminous fog costume would allow.

Cheeks burning, she reached the open field at the edge of the foggy activities. This time she felt grateful for the heavy mist that shrouded her from prying eyes until she could stop trembling.

Maude greeted her with a camera in her hand and outrage in her eyes. "Where in the world have you been? And where is your hat?"

"Er, I couldn't find it."

"Oh, for crying out loud. Never mind, we'll take the pictures without it." She bustled the waiting crowd of three into a tidy line. "Are you catching something,

Ruth? Your face is flushed."

"Must be all the excitement." Several yards away, a hot air balloon was fully inflated.

Thanks to Maude's ruthless management, the children were all photographed in under an hour. By then, the Phineas Phogg balloon was aloft, floating upward with graceful ease, the rainbow stripes vivid against the blue sky. Ruth could see the propane flame strengthen as a man fired the burner. At first she thought it was Bing, but the hair color was wrong.

Ed Honeysill's wide face peered over the side of the basket as he waved to the crowd gathered below. Then he straightened and shaded his eyes with his hands, taking in the view.

As they drifted farther aloft, three men below monitored the ropes anchoring the balloon to the ground.

Ruth craned her neck to watch until her sinews began to protest. Suddenly a terrific bang cut through the crowd noise.

A dark spot raced its way through the sky, trailed by a stream of light and smoke. It ripped into the side of the balloon and tore a hole in one of the bright green stripes before exiting out a red one.

The balloon rocked violently to one side and then the other before the nylon burst into flames. The men on the ground stood in dumb surprise, holding the ropes slack for a moment before they snapped into action, desperately trying to haul the balloon earthward. One of the two figures in the basket leaped, falling directly on top of the inflated jump house and rolling off onto the grass.

Suddenly the burning side of the balloon disintegrated. The basket rocketed to one side. The second man flew out of the basket and flailed to the ground, landing with a thud at the edge of the clearing.

Ruth closed her mouth with a snap. "Call 911!" she yelled. She yanked the giant disks off her torso and started to run.

Maude struggled to dial and run at the same time.

They reached the spot and wheezed to a halt, panting and uncertain. The second man's limbs were splayed out in a windmill fashion around his body. The back of his head lay exposed, like a shiny white mushroom emerging from the soil.

It became sickeningly clear that there was no life in Ed's body, but Ruth forced herself to check for a pulse on the wrist closest to her.

Maude clicked off the phone and looked at her. "Is he dead?"

She nodded, swallowing her revulsion. Maude nodded back. "Okay. We'll keep people away until the authorities arrive." Though Maude's voice was steady, Ruth could feel a shock and horror radiating out of her that mirrored her own feelings.

A woman with stylish and familiar turquoise sandals came flying up to them. She stopped short when they moved closely together to prevent her from seeing beyond them.

"Candace," Ruth said gently, "I think you'd better sit down."

3

Jack rode with Nate and Mary to a hole-in-the-wall up the coast called Wings and Things. Not the classiest ambiance, but free nachos during the pre-lunch hours. He went with reluctance. It didn't seem particularly important for the Finny police detective to celebrate his thirty-fifth birthday. The night before, the babysitter helped his almost-four-year-old son, Paul, bake a lopsided cake, decorated with sugar letters spelling out HAPPY BIRTHDAY ADDY since Paul had consumed one too many *d*'s.

Jack didn't make much fuss about his birthday, maybe because his wife had died two days before his thirty-third. The sweater she intended to give him hung unworn in the closet next to his dress uniform. He remembered her holding it against herself when she didn't know he was looking, checking it for size. For some reason, he couldn't wear it or give it away. But sometimes, very late at night, he would smell the fabric, trying to catch the faintest whisper of her scent that had long ago evaporated.

It seemed important to his colleagues to buy him lunch on his birthday, so he plastered a smile on his face and allowed himself to be shanghaied. Besides, it gave them a chance to skip town for a few hours after the parade took place. Yolo, the newest officer, was left to maintain a police presence at the precinct.

The place smelled like wet carpet and stale cologne.

Jack nursed a club soda, not only because they technically were still on duty, but because he'd long ago decided that drinking and raising toddlers did not complement each other. Mary Dirisi was trying to teach fellow officer Nathan Katz how to throw darts. Nate's throws wound up rattling to the floor, or they got stuck in the plant next to the men's room door. Jack wondered how anyone with that kind of aim passed the qualifications on the police firing range. Nevertheless, although Nathan couldn't throw a dart worth a hoot, he was one of the few people Jack would trust with his life.

Jack's thoughts strayed to the toe. The lab could contribute nothing more than to confirm that yes, it was indeed a toe from an adult male human, and it had been severed within the past two days. So far no one hobbled forward to claim it, and the rest of the body formerly attached to the toe had not been found, either. It was weird, but in Finny, weird was not uncommon. As a matter of fact, since the festival had begun to attract people from everywhere, weird was getting positively commonplace.

Jack had spent the morning listening to Alva Hernandez spouting a tale about a bunch of murderous proctologists. Alva was convinced there was some sort of plot brewing at the top of Finny's Nose. The last time he filed a report with the Finny police, it had to do with the Loch Ness monster, which he was dead sure had holed up in Tookie Newsome's trout pond for the winter.

In the name of community outreach, Jack had driven upslope with Alva and examined the area. There was nothing much to find, only a few bits of wire on a grassy plateau bordered by an army of cedar and sycamore trees. Nothing much, but something did bother the detective about it. It didn't seem like the doings of the local kids looking for a place to make trouble. Something about Alva's story felt foreign, alien to the seaside town.

His thoughts wandered back to the present. With his back to the wall, he noticed a small woman a couple of tables over, sipping a glass of water. She was interesting— short dark hair, the tiniest hands he had ever seen, a dreamy look on her freckled face. She was not beautiful in the magazine-cover sense, too strong a chin, too round a face. Her sandal bobbed up and down over her crossed knee, as if she was tired of waiting for someone. A man in cowboy clothes sauntered up to her.

"Come on, Jack. Relax already. This is supposed to be a celebration, remember?" Mary plopped down next to him with a plate of steaming nachos. "I've given up on this idiot." She gestured to an approaching Nate. "He's the worst dart player on the planet."

Nate huffed into his mustache. "Yeah, well, I play a mean game of Candyland."

As the father of five girls, including five-year-old triplets, Nathan Katz was a man of infinite patience and an absolute whiz at dressing Barbie dolls, tiny stiletto heels and all.

"You've got to start beefing up your testosterone. You spend too much time surrounded by women," Mary said. She flipped her braid over her shoulder for emphasis.

"It's true," Nate agreed. "I'm pretty sure even our goldfish is a female. It's got kind of girly flippers."

"Goldfish don't have flippers," she said as she reached for a gooey nacho.

"Spoken like someone who needs a pet in their life."

"I'm considering getting one."

"I hear spider monkeys like strong female companionship," Nate said. A slug of melted cheese dropped onto his shirtfront.

"I was thinking more along the lines of canine, you toad."

Jack listened to their banter with one ear and simultaneously eavesdropped on the conversation at another table. The cowboy was making himself friendly.

"Actually, I'm waiting for someone, but thanks anyway," the small woman said, putting down her glass.

The guy, complete with pointy boots and enormous belt buckle, laid a smooth hand on her table. The creases in his plaid shirt labeled him more familiar with department stores than the wide-open range.

"You're much too good-looking to be left alone here," he breathed. "Some guy doesn't know what he's doin' leaving you by yourself."

"Thanks for the attention, really, but I am not interested in company. Why don't you go find another 'gal' to talk to, okay?" She smiled as she said the words.

"Awww, you don't really mean that, darling."

Jack put down his club soda and pushed out his chair a fraction. Mary and Nate grew quiet as they picked up on his tension.

The cowboy grabbed hold of her slender wrist. "Come on, honey, I'll show you how to loosen up." He pulled her out of her chair and yanked her to his chest.

By the time Jack and the others made it to their feet, the woman had kneed the drunken man in the groin, whacked the back of his head as he bent over in pain, and shoved him to the ground. Then she stood with a sandal planted firmly above his collar, her little painted toenails bright against the man's sweaty neck.

Bending down close to his face, she said calmly, "The next time a woman says no, maybe you should consider the possibility that she really means it." She picked up her purse, dropped a few bills on the table, and walked out of the bar.

Jack, Nate, and Mary stood in openmouthed astonishment.

"Man," Nate said.

"Man, oh man," Mary echoed.

Jack's legs seemed to work of their own accord. He was on his way to the door, following the woman, when his pager began to vibrate. Checking the screen, he muttered under his breath and took out his cell phone.

After a minute he said, "We've gotta go. Problem at the festival. Thanks for the birthday lunch, guys. Time to get back to work."

They paid the check and headed out the door as the humiliated cowboy slunk back to his buddies.

Out in the parking lot, there was no sign of her in the swirling fog.

4

If Cootchie was born under an unlucky star, it certainly didn't show on the surface.

She was a wild-haired, button-nosed preschooler, with chubby legs constantly engaged in a gallop. She would have been born into a privileged life if her wealthy grandfather had accepted her paternity. She should have been the object of adoration of her maternal grandmother if the woman hadn't abandoned her own child decades before. As it was, she was the daughter of a man who had been murdered before she showed up on a sonogram, the child of a mother prone to speaking in fortune cookie vernacular.

It was still a subject of wonder to Ruth that she had ever become part of this odd woman's life. She finally concluded that it was due to a stark vulnerability both women experienced at the same time, the murder of Dimple's lover, and Ruth's complete loss of identity and purpose after her beloved husband's death.

That and the murderer running rampant in Finny. Somehow, out of the chaos, God brought them together.

And now the chaos had returned, or so it seemed. Ruth's muscles ached from the wild sprint to the crash site the previous day. Poor, poor Ed. She felt queasy just thinking about the way his life abruptly ended. She had not slept well, tossing and turning, even after Monk prepared her a middle-of-the-night cup of tea.

The early morning was cold, heavy with fog. Cootchie twirled madly in Ruth's backyard, hands up in the air as the gulls circled around her and stabbed orange beaks into her pockets, looking for goldfish crackers. "Whee! Whee!" she squealed.

Somewhere in mid-twirl, one of the gulls succeeded in knocking the girl over, causing her to scrape her knee. She put her chubby fists to her eyes and whimpered. Ruth shooed the birds away and sat down with Cootchie on the porch steps.

"Did those mean birds knock you over, Cootchie? Let Nana Ruth see that scrape." She found the knee free from blood and gave her a hug, relishing her sweet-smelling hair and the chubby arms around her neck. The child's cheeks were cold from the morning chill.

She flashed back to the day Cootchie was born. It had been a frantic drive to Eden Hospital in the middle of the night; at the hospital, Dimple was stuck in a nonproductive labor that lasted three days. By the time the baby was finally coaxed into the world, poor Dimple was mentally and physically depleted. A chipper nurse handed the new mother a form to fill out for the birth certificate. Ruth could still see the nurse's frown as she handed it back to Dimple after scanning the paper.

"Are you sure the name is, er, spelled correctly and everything? That's just the way you want it?" the nurse had asked.

Dimple nodded wearily and fell asleep.

It wasn't until several hours later that baby Cootchie was returned to her mother's room and Ruth learned the infant's name.

"Dimple, uh, is Cootchie a family name?"

"No, it just came to me," Dimple said before falling asleep again.

Ruth joggled the baby for an hour, walking her in circles around the room, before she noticed the package of Cootchie Coo diapers on the counter at the foot of Dimple's bed.

It's a good thing they weren't Poopy Poo diapers.

She pulled her mind away from the fond memories. The girl was asleep with her first two fingers jammed into her mouth. Her hair collected in wild, sweaty spirals the color of a rusty nail.

Could anything be more soothing than holding a sleeping child? Ruth could vaguely remember rocking her only son when he was an infant. Bryce had been a crabby infant, colicky, the doctors said; but he'd put up with her tentative mothering skills just fine. As he grew, his independent personality was a source of confusion to her. Most of the memories from his early school years were of him pushing her away, rejecting her affection, physical and otherwise. She did not understand why their relationship was so distant, why it had always been that way. At this point, she was pretty sure she never would.

"He needs to go his own way," Phillip had said many times. "Some people are like that."

Bryce had finally landed in Chicago and now lived a separate life, married to Roslyn, with no children. Except for the obligatory phone call on her birthday, she never heard from him. Bryce had revered his father, but even at Phillip's funeral he was unable to express his feelings of loss to her. They stayed safe, discussing practical matters and the weather until he flew back home after the memorial service.

Cootchie stirred and blinked her eyes. "Where's Papa Monk?"

"He's at work, sweet pea. We'll see him later." She wished he were home. They had stayed up late into the night discussing the disaster. The police said it was a flare gun that took the balloon down, and Ed along with it.

She still had the images burned into her retinas: a haggard-faced Candace collapsed on the ground, Bing bent over her. The whole scene replayed itself in her mind.

She recalled Alva watching the proceedings with a puff of blue cotton candy clutched in his fist, and a wide-eyed Hugh arriving posthaste to the crash site with a host of other festivalgoers.

Then there was an infiltration of police and fire personnel that seemed to drift in and out of focus. They were focused intently on their individual duties, unaffected by the horror around them. Jack Denny talked into a radio as Nathan and Mary staked an area around the gore with yellow tape.

Jack had spoken to his officers in a low tone. "Check out the insurance situation—beneficiaries and such."

Monk materialized next to Ruth and wrapped her in a massive hug. "Are you okay? I heard a horrendous bang, so I locked up the store and came running." He looked into her eyes. "Is that a body over there? What happened? Are you hurt, honey?"

"No." The worry in his gray eyes filled her heart. She leaned her head for a moment into his garlic-scented embrace. Her words trickled out, faltering, uncertain. "There was a flash of something across the sky. A shot of some sort, and then the balloon caught fire and just sort of dissolved. They tried to get it down, but they couldn't do it in time. Ed Honeysill, he—fell out of the basket." She watched the paramedics load Candace up in the ambulance. "He's dead, I'm pretty sure. I can't believe it. It happened in a blink."

His embrace tightened. "What a thing for you to see. I never should have let you out the door this morning." He rested his cheek on the top of her head.

Bing approached then, his muscular arms folded against his broad chest. "It was a flare gun."

"How do you know?" Monk asked.

"I know a flare when I see it," he snapped. "It was fired at pretty close range, too. Maybe a couple hundred feet, I'd say." Bing shook his head. "That's an eight-thousand-dollar balloon. Just look at it."

"Yes," Monk said, "and a pretty big inconvenience to the passengers, not to mention the witnesses."

Bing looked at him sharply. "I almost lost one of my guys, too. He landed on the jump house. Just sprained an ankle and didn't flatten any kids in the process."

Jack had joined them at that point. "Mr. Mitchell, we're going to need to talk to you about what happened. Would you mind giving some information to Officer Katz over there?"

Bing strode off.

"Are you two doing all right?" Jack asked. When they nodded, he added, "I'm afraid this means a trip down to the office, Ruth. Can I schedule you for an interview tomorrow, maybe?" His brown eyes were soft.

She nodded.

Nathan walked up with two plastic bags in his rubber-gloved hands. "That's all we've got."

One bag held a bulky gun with a wide barrel and the other a twisted metal eyeglass frame.

Jack asked Monk to escort Ruth home.

Tucked into Monk's strong arm, she had made her way downslope. As they walked, a thought froze in her brain. If the flare was indeed fired at close range, then someone in Finny's swirling fog was a murderer.

And he was close.

Very close.

The thought made her shiver once again.

Now, as Ruth sat on the porch step trying to puzzle out who would have wanted to kill Ed Honeysill, Cootchie awakened and interrupted her reverie.

"Go park? With Paul?"

"We can go to the park, honey, but Mr. Denny said Paul has to go to the doctor today. Maybe we can play with him tomorrow. We can go for a little while before I take you home. Can you help me feed the worms first?"

Ruth took a minute to slide the solar panels off the eight-foot-long concrete beds, ignoring the ache in her left calf. Phillip had come up with the vermiculture idea, figuring it would be a unique business venture and a good supplement to the birds' diet of protein pellets and whatever they could lay their beaks on. He'd finished constructing the beds and ordered a starter supply of worms before he came across the fact that worms need to be kept in a cozy sixty-to-seventy-degree range. Hence the construction of the solar panels, which served not only to keep the worms happy but to keep the birds out. Worms were pretty easygoing critters unless the temperature got too hot. Only once did Ruth have to worry about the wigglers overheating. The weather in Finny topped one hundred about as often as Comet Hale-Bopp whizzed overhead.

Cootchie held the box of litmus strips while Ruth did a quick reading and found the pH to be a healthy 7.1. She shoveled a modest quantity of bird manure onto the top of the beds, and the child danced along beside her sprinkling the top with shredded paper.

She replaced the solar panels and grabbed her travel kit. The cameras and extra film it used to contain had given way to boxes of organic carrot juice, edamame, and toddler-sized overalls. She laughed to herself. "What a difference a year makes."

Beams of light made ghostly patches of sun and shadow but did nothing to dispel the chill from their fingers and toes as they walked. It was a gentle downhill trudge from Ruth's cottage to the park in the center of town. The sun was trying to burrow its way through the fog when they arrived. Along the way, they were treated to the sight of rolling seas of yellow mustard flower and patches of spiky artichokes that grew wild along the walking trail. Ruth was once again grateful for the rippled foothills that formed an uneven border almost completely around the rear of the mountain called Finny's Nose. They were just too topographically uncooperative to allow for much building development in the shadow of the nose.

She could hear the faraway strains of festival music. Finny Park was a small grassy area plopped without much planning or forethought in the town square. Blowing on her hands to warm them, she led Cootchie to the steps of a rickety slide. The girl climbed to the top of the steps and shouted, "Mara!" pointing to a spot behind Ruth.

It was indeed Martha, the escape artist bird, hobbling up behind her, quick in spite of the missing wing. "How do you *do* that?" Ruth muttered.

Martha had been given to Ruth's husband with a plastic six-pack ring embedded in her neck feathers, which had no doubt made her easy prey for the cat that maimed her. Phillip surmised that she had gotten tangled up in it as a very young bird and it began to slowly strangle her as she grew, leaving her, if not brain damaged, then certainly with a heavy dose of goofiness. It was theoretically possible that Martha could fly if she had the gumption to try. In her five years with Ruth, she never had.

Martha darted around the bench, attempting to rifle through the travel kit, when Hugh Lemmon approached carrying a cardboard box. The shy, gangly man nodded his head in a hello; then in mid-nod, he tripped over the leg of the park bench. He caught himself, but not before the contents of the box tumbled to the ground.

"Are you okay, Hugh?"

His eyes widened in alarm as Martha scuttled around, chasing the rolling black objects.

"Stop!" he yelled, leaping after her. "Don't let her eat those." He made it to the bird before Ruth did, grabbing her around the neck and prying the blob from her mouth. "Hold on to her until I pick them up," he said.

He poked around in the grass and under the bench, gently retrieving the items from where they had landed. Hugh had an impressive beaklike nose and looked not a little birdlike himself as he bobbed up and down on skinny legs. His chin and forehead sloped away from his prodigious schnoz as though to escape to lower altitudes. When he finished, he walked back over to Ruth, cradling the box in his arms.

"I was thinking about the balloon crash instead of watching where I was going," he said.

"Did any of your, er, whatever those are, get broken?"

He held up one of the black lumps and inspected it. "No, doesn't look like it. No harm done, I think."

"Hugh, I've just got to ask. What is that? It looks kind of like—"

"Poo poo!" Cootchie screamed gleefully from her perch at the top of the slide.

Ruth reddened, but she could see the child's point. Resting between his long fingers was a warty, lopsided wad, the color of the chocolate pudding she would never admit she'd eaten for breakfast.

Hugh laughed. His prominent teeth winked in

the sunlight. "I know it's not that attractive to most people, but to many it's more mesmerizing than gold. It's a *Tuber melanosporum*. Otherwise known as a black truffle."

"Really? I've never actually seen one. I only recently learned on the Food Channel that the underground ones are different from the chocolate ones."

"The candy variety got their name because their small round shape resembled the tuberous ones."

"Tuffles, muffles, muffins, tuffets," Cootchie sang from the top of the slide.

"Where did you get them?" Ruth asked.

He gazed at the truffle fondly. "These beauties came from southwestern France."

"That's a long way to go for a little morsel."

"That's true. Oh, they've begun to farm truffles here and there, Texas and Oregon, but they are not of the same quality. Wild truffles go for up to four hundred fifty dollars a pound."

Ruth's jaw dropped. "A *pound*?"

Hugh nodded. "You betcha. I'm working out a deal with a supplier in France. He sends me as many pounds as he can find, and I sell them to the West Coast market. They're starving for the really good truffles here."

"Is that profitable?" Ruth asked after recovering use of her mandible.

"It will be. People here are willing to pay an extra fee for not having to deal with buying and shipping the truffles themselves. This is going to be a real moneymaker. I've even got a deal pending with a small charter plane company to fly them up and down the coast for me, and I've almost got my Web site up and running."

"That's really great. What exactly does a truffle taste like?"

"It's unlike anything you've ever experienced." Hugh pushed his glasses farther up his nose. "It's kind of musky, with a taste of nuts and ozone."

Ruth failed in her attempt to imagine what a nutty ozone flavor would be like. "Your father must be excited about it."

Hugh lived with his father, Royland Lemmon, who operated a very successful organic farm on the outskirts of Finny, specializing in field greens. Ruth had met him years before when she'd gone with Phillip to assist his examination of Royland's pig, Noodles. Noodles tipped the scales at eight hundred twenty-three pounds. Prior to the veterinary exam, she cocked her piggish snout, widened beady brown eyes, and fell deeply in love with Phillip. She dogged his every step, snuffling at the back of his hands when he left them within range and generally showering him with enough piggy adoration to bring a blush to Phillip's cheeks.

Hugh placed the truffle back into the box. "Dad's not involved. He doesn't understand moving with the times. He'll be growing arugula for the rest of his life."

"His arugula is wonderful, though," she said. It was, too. Pungent and crisp with a peppery bite. Nothing ozonish about it.

"Yes, it is. I can't argue with that. Dad's offering

free tours of the farm for Fog Festival attendees this weekend. If there are any."

"Hopefully there will be a good crowd, in spite of the, er, accident."

Hugh nodded. "Yeah. Who would have imagined that happening in Finny? A guy killed right in front of everybody."

"I know." Ruth shook her head. "I still can't get over it. One minute Ed is alive, and the next. . ."

"He's spread all over."

She swallowed hard and nodded.

"Down, peese." Cootchie could never quite be convinced to slide down the slide once she got to the top.

"I've got to get this young lady home to her mother. I'm glad my feathered friend didn't cause any damage. I'll be eager to see your Web site when it's on its feet. Give my love to your father. And Noodles, of course."

Ruth lifted Cootchie down. "And good luck with your truffle business."

Hugh waved and continued on his way.

As Ruth packed up the child and her belongings, she noticed a stray black lump nestled at the edge of grass and sand. "Looks like he missed one."

Martha looked disappointed as Ruth slid the truffle into the pocket of her sweater. "At four hundred fifty dollars a pound," she said to the bird, "you're sticking to onion rings."

The twosome made their way from the park to Dimple's house. It was still chilly, but sunlight stabbed through pockets in the fog, dazzling their eyes as it bounced off the white stucco buildings of downtown.

Ruth loved the intensely green leaves of the old trees that poked up in between the buildings. The sweet smell from the far-off fields of ornamental flowers drifted in and out of her consciousness. She gazed at Vern Rosario's stand of trees on the distant horizon. Sad to think that he would be cutting them down soon to accommodate his new barn.

A half hour later, Ruth and Cootchie were walking past the Dent mansion on their way to Dimple's cottage. Though the cantankerous Buster Dent refused to acknowledge his daughter and granddaughter, he allowed them to remain in the small home that Dimple's mother had decorated before she ran off with a visiting investment banker. Buster could not forgive Dimple for her affair with Finny's curator anymore than he could forgive his own cheating wife.

He was a hard man. Ruth had a feeling he had been that way even before his wife's desertion. Now he was wealthy from selling his vast acres of pumpkin farm to a developer. But despite his wealth, he was alone, as far as anyone could tell. Occasionally, though, as she herded Cootchie home, she had the uncanny feeling that someone was watching through the upstairs window of the patriarch's home. Someone who watched the little girl as she trotted happily along, filling her pockets with feathers and pebbles. This feeling kept Ruth from despising Buster completely. She knew what it was like to watch life from the outside in, to see love and warmth through an unforgiving pane of separation. She reminded herself to add him to her prayers.

And Meg. She should pray for Meg. Why did

the thought of Dimple's estranged mother make her stomach knot?

After a deep breath, she knocked gently and ushered Cootchie into the bright kitchen. "Dimple," she called. "We're home. Are you here?" She waited, fearing she would hear Meg's voice. After a moment, she relaxed. Dimple's mother wasn't there.

She heard Dimple call from somewhere in the back.

"Just a minute," Ruth called back. "I can't hear you. Let me get Cootchie her snack and I'll be right there."

She poured a glass of pomegranate juice for the child. Once again the thought occurred to her that Cootchie must be the only almost-three-year-old in the world to have pomegranate juice and soybeans for a snack.

Ruth walked down the hall and through the sitting room, stepping over boxes of dusty books and papers stacked dizzily on the Persian rug.

"Where are you, Dimple?" she called again. A faint voice answered, but she could not make out the words. "What?" she yelled.

Cootchie trotted out into the sitting room, lugging a tattered copy of her favorite book. "Read, peese."

"Oh, all right. I guess your mommy is busy with something. Climb aboard." Ruth hauled Dimple into her lap. A few muscles complained as she did so.

The girl settled in her lap and opened the slim volume.

"So from the mould, Scarlet and Gold,
Many a Bulb will rise
Hidden away, cunningly, from sagacious eyes."

Cootchie's unusual reading habits began almost from birth. It had simply never occurred to Dimple that a young child might prefer hearing about a large purple dinosaur or a cat in a striped hat rather than the great works of the romantic poets. When the pediatrician advised her to read quality books to her baby, she took the suggestion to heart, immediately setting out to the bookstore and returning with *The Norton Anthology of Poetry*, as well as the *Iliad* and the *Odyssey* and *The Mill on the Floss* for good measure. Ruth was hoping they could delay the George Eliot novel until Cootchie was at least four. That would give her time to read the CliffsNotes.

After a few more verses, Cootchie noticed the stacked boxes and toddled off to the pile and returned momentarily with a dingy leather-bound journal.

"Read, peese."

"What is this? I'm not sure Mommy meant for us to read this, honey. How about some Frost?"

Undeterred, the girl continued to hold the book out. "Read, peese."

She sighed. "All right, but if this is Faust, I'm out of here."

The writing was a lovely, loopy script, faded in places but for the most part legible.

August the third, 1923

    Trouble tonight. A big bear of a man came in from San Francisco, one of Slats' boys. He said someone jumped him and stole the cash bag. No good will come of this, I know. Anyone who crosses Slats, does so at his own peril.

Ruth's voice trailed off after the first sentence, leaving Cootchie disgusted enough to hop off her lap and sit down to play with blocks.

I got a new piano man for the dining hall. He does some nice ragtime tunes. The showgirls like his playing and folks enjoy the music, which gives me a chance to sell more Apple Bettys.

"What in the world is this?" Ruth said aloud. Was it really a journal from 1923?

Suddenly a head popped out of the ceiling.

"Greetings, Ruth."

Ruth launched the journal into the air and yelped. The upside-down face trailed a blond curtain of hair. "What are you doing up there?"

"I'm sorry," Dimple said from the attic opening. "You said you wanted some old pictures of Finny, so I ventured into the attic. Do you want some iced tea?"

"Do you have any up there?"

"No. I would need to come down to find the tea."

Humor was hit or miss with Dimple. "Don't bother."

"No bother. A friend is a raft over the troubled waters of life."

"Er, yes. Well, don't launch the raft; I'll just get some myself."

Ruth chuckled as she headed toward the kitchen, pondering the wisdom of a woman who used to write fortunes for a living. She filled a glass half full of dark brown tea and added water. Dimple's homemade tea blends produced a liquid that could only be likened to drinking potpourri. Extra water and lots of ice made it more palatable.

Dimple materialized in the kitchen. She brushed her hands on the front of her long skirt. "Tell me about your day, Ruth, dear," she said.

"Maude called to tell me crowds are really thin today at the festival. Probably due to the accident."

Dimple nodded. "What a tragic thing. Grief is a heavy weight to bear."

Ruth wondered how heavy it would be for the widowed Candace. "I managed to avoid any morning festival duties, so Cootchie and I played with the birds, and then we went to the park. We saw Hugh there. Did you know he's going into the truffle importing business?"

She blinked. "The tuberous ones?"

"The black, wrinkly kind that pigs eat. I discovered that Martha has a taste for them, too. But about this journal." She held the volume up for inspection. "What is this? Where did you get it?"

"From the attic. You said you wanted some authentic Finny historical documents for the booklet you're creating. I think these are authentic. They were in amongst some old photos that belonged to Grandpa Dent. I've never looked at the things before."

Ruth opened the book again. "The date is 1923, and the name on the 'Belongs to' page is Pickles Peckenpaugh. Does that name ring a bell?"

Dimple shook her head. "What is the book about?"

"From what I gather in the first entry, the woman runs a restaurant."

"That wasn't uncommon during Prohibition. Many were run by women. It was one of the few ways they could achieve economic empowerment."

"How do you know all that?"

"I know a few things besides how to grow mushrooms."

"Do you mind if I borrow this journal for a while? Ellen Foots gives presentations on Finny history to the schoolkids. Maybe I can ask her about it."

Dimple rubbed her nose. "Be my guest. Thank you for watching Cootchie for me today."

"My pleasure." Ruth watched the child peering at the carpet fibers through a magnifying glass.

"We're going to go pick some nettles for stewing after her nap."

Stewed nettles. Ruth nodded, wondering how Cootchie would be accepted in life by other children who didn't know nettles from noodles. By now, Ruth had learned not to ask.

"Okeydokey. Do you need anything else for Monday's birthday party?" It seemed strange to be celebrating anything on the heels of Ed's death, but Cootchie was looking forward to her special day.

"No, thank you. We're going to make the cake together tomorrow. Jack has volunteered to barbecue. It's his birthday celebration, too."

It remained to be seen if Jack would appreciate a hefty piece of carrot cake with tofu frosting, or even if he'd be able to spare any time away from work to eat it. "I can't believe she is going to be three. Where did the time go?"

Dimple smiled dreamily. "Time is our most patient friend and restive enemy."

When would Dimple run out of fortunes? She'd been away from the fortune cookie business for two years, and so far no sign that the stream of Zen wisdom was drying up. Ruth tried to figure out a way to bring up the subject she had been dreading. "It was a surprise to see your mother."

"For me, too," Dimple said.

"So are you—? How are things going? Between you?"

Dimple cocked her head to the side, green eyes thoughtful. "About as well as they should, I think."

"Oh." Ruth wanted to ask questions, to clarify, to ease her mind. Instead, she waited to see if she would add any more pertinent details.

"Would you mind bringing a bucket of castings if you've got any? My zinnia bed needs coddling now," Dimple said.

There was to be no mind-easing at this time. "Sure thing. Chips and dip and worm castings. I'll be here around six on Monday." She looked at her watch. "Oh boy. I've gotta get to the shop to help Monk."

Ruth kissed Cootchie and hurried down the walkway, eager to get home. She had a feeling Pickles Peckenpaugh had a lot more story to tell.

5

Monk whistled cheerfully as he hauled a twenty-pound sack of risotto rice over the threshold of Monk's Coffee and Catering. Ruth admired the easy way her new husband lifted the heavy bundle. An ex–navy man, he was built like a walk-in freezer. Everything from his head down to his booted feet was roughly squarish as opposed to her roundish.

He had a temper, and definite opinions where patriotism and morality were concerned. He was so very strong, yet so completely tender with her. He treated her like a delicate crystal glass that might chip at any moment. His devotion still amazed her.

At the moment, his cheeks were flushed with exertion. "You look like an angel," he said.

She laughed and kissed him before wiping up the puddle of milk on the stainless steel counter. "Are you sure you aren't just saying that to keep me on for the afternoon shift?" She manned the counter for a few hours to provide assistance for the caffeine-deprived folks arriving late in the day to participate in the festival.

"No way, ma'am. I never could resist a woman wearing an apron."

She blushed, feeling like a silly schoolgirl. Or maybe, she thought, like a newlywed. "You know that sort of remark can get you into trouble now. Women don't like to be seen in aprons these days. It's not very politically correct."

He nodded forlornly. "Don't I know it. They all want to be toting pistols or pagers. It's a strange world."

She knew that he did not comprehend the whims of the younger generation, particularly the female members. He was sometimes rendered speechless by the teen girls who came into the shop with belly rings exposed and profanity spilling from their glossed lips. She wondered what Monk would think of Candace.

"And getting stranger all the time." She shuddered, thinking about the balloon crash.

He took hold of her hand. "How are you doing with, you know, the crash? Feel any better?"

"I was hoping I would snap out of it and find it was all a terrible dream." She shook her head. "I still can't believe it."

"Me neither. I can't believe we're still going forward with this nutty festival after what happened."

"Nothing short of nuclear war would keep Maude from fulfilling her festival dreams," Ruth said as she refilled a thermos with cream. "I just hope nothing else happens. I'm still wondering how come no one has found the rest of—you know—what was attached to the toe." The thought made Ruth feel squirmy.

"Can't begin to guess. I hear the police have had the dogs out sniffing down nose, but they haven't found any more digits to speak of." He put a tray of scones into the oven.

"Have you heard anything about a gang?"

"No." He closed the oven door with a bang. "Only what Alva has been going on about. Of course, I've been preoccupied thinking about Bobby."

She smiled. He was so excited that his niece was coming to visit. It had been all he could talk about recently.

The bell over the door tinkled as Detective Jack Denny entered.

"Morning, Monk. Hello, Ruth," Jack said before plopping into a scarred wooden chair. His face was stained with fatigue, and there was a sprinkling of dark stubble on his chin.

"Long day?" she asked.

"Uh–huh, and it's not over yet."

Ruth wanted to tell Jack about what she had overheard in the trailer before Ed's death, but she didn't want to be a gossip. *It's not gossip,* she reminded herself, *when a murder is involved.* Perhaps Candace had already told him. No, she didn't think that was likely. She decided she would tell the detective. She was ready to grill him right then about any further developments relating to the balloon crash, but the exhaustion on his face took the wind out of her nosey sails.

He looked as tired as she felt.

Aside from Ed's horrible death, another kernel of unease settled into her stomach, refusing to be dislodged. The feeling, Ruth was forced to acknowledge, was jealousy, pure and simple. She had spent a restless night contemplating the sudden arrival of Dimple's long-absent mother. The most irritating thing about Meg Sooner was that she appeared to be a genuinely nice person, from the few bits she'd gleaned from Dimple since the woman arrived. The feelings that rose in her own heart were far from nice. Those "deeds of the flesh" seemed to unroll in her mind, starting with jealousy and working through strife, disputes, and the illustrious envy.

The Post-it in her pocket bore her scribbled reminder: *Fruit of the Spirit.*

Love. Joy. Peace. Patience. Kindness. Goodness. Faithfulness. Gentleness. Self-control. Since Meg had showed up, Ruth didn't feel as though she was bearing much fruit at all, especially in the kindness and goodness department. She pushed the image of the small, well-manicured woman out of her mind.

"I've always maintained these long days would be so much easier for people if they didn't start so early," she said.

"Amen to that," Jack said. "It doesn't help that the coffee machine at the station is on the fritz again. I'm beginning to think the thing goes out every time someone sneezes."

"Well, if you don't want any latte, frappe, mocha thingy, I can help you with that," she said, grabbing a styrofoam cup. "I only know how to pour it straight from the pot."

"Perfect. Straight from the pot, to go, please."

Monk called over her shoulder, "How about a side of banana muffin? I made some fresh this morning. There are still a few left, I think."

Jack closed his eyes. "Coffee and carbohydrates. Sounds like a balanced meal to me. You don't have a pound of sausage to round it out, do you?"

"I'm afraid not," Ruth laughed as she prepared his order. "Paul and Cootchie had a blast last week. The birds are still lying around the yard this morning, too pooped to function."

"I hope he didn't hurt any of them."

"You know very well my birds are the toughest pets on the block." She poured out some steaming coffee. "All the neighborhood dogs and cats are petrified of them."

"Yes." Jack's brown eyes sparkled. "I remember having a knock-down-drag-out with one of them on your front lawn. I'm still not sure which one of us won."

Jack and Ruth had become friends after the sudden death of his young wife, Lacey. Following the tragedy, his two-year-old son had become selectively mute, refusing to communicate with anyone except their wild, rambunctious dog Mr. Boo Boo. Somehow Paul made a sort of connection with Ruth's flock of gulls that had begun to draw him out of his shell. Paul was not verbose by any means, but at the age of four, he was beginning to string a few words together. Either Jack or Louella, Paul's nanny, brought Paul by as often as possible to play with the birds and with Cootchie Dent. What with a yard full of gimpy birds, vats full of worms, and a little girl to play with, the Budge backyard was better than Disneyland.

As Jack inhaled coffee vapors, Monk finished unloading the last of his deliveries.

"Wonderful. She's here," he said, glancing out the window. "I wanted both of you to meet my niece. She's going to be helping me out for a while until these two weeks of Fog Festival stuff are over." He held the door open for a tiny dark-haired woman.

Jack knocked his cup of coffee onto the floor. He stood up, a dark patch of coffee soaked into the knee of his pants.

Monk planted a kiss on the woman's cheek and enveloped her in a smothering hug. "This is my favorite niece, Bobby Walker."

"I'm your only niece, Uncle Monk."

"No matter. You'd be my favorite even if I had a passel of them. I'd like you to meet Ruth, my amazing wife and the woman who is keeping me afloat."

Ruth clasped Bobby's hands in her own. "It's so wonderful to finally meet you."

"And you, Ruth." Bobby smiled back.

"And this fella with the coffee all over himself is Jack Denny, one of Finny's finest," Monk finished.

The woman turned her curious black gaze on him.

Jack recovered himself enough to reply. "Actually, we almost met before."

Bobby tilted her head. "We did?"

"Yes. I was at a place up the coast, Wings and Things. You were there waiting for someone, I think, and a fellow with a cowboy hat wanted to get chummy."

She thought for a minute. "Oh, right. I was waiting for this big lug, as a matter of fact." She stabbed a thumb at Monk.

Monk frowned. "That's the day my van had a flat. I couldn't reach you on your cell. I must have called fifty times and it said 'not in service.'" His eyes rounded in horror. "Did some guy harass you?"

"I don't think you've got anything to worry

about," Jack said. "The lady seems to be able to handle herself."

"I'm a park ranger, and I've driven a school bus in east LA, among other things. I'm pretty hard to scare. I don't remember noticing you. Oh, wait a minute. Were you watching a man play darts? A guy who couldn't hit the broad side of a barn?"

"That would be my buddy Nate Katz. His incompetence with darts is legendary." He took some paper napkins from the counter and knelt to mop up the spilled coffee. "Are you vacationing here?"

"Sort of an imposed one. The park service is insisting we take our vacation days whether we like it or not. It seemed like a good time to hit the beach. Besides, I love the coast this time of year. Lots of fog and everything coming back to life."

"Where are you staying?" Jack asked.

"At the hotel. Uncle Monk wanted me to stay at the cottage, but three's a crowd."

The front doorbell tinkled, and a crowd of work-men came in. They were noisily discussing the plans to tape off a field for festival parking purposes. Bobby laughed, taking an apron from a peg on the wall. "So much for vacation. Okay, Mrs. Budge, you'd better show me the ropes posthaste."

"Please call me Ruth," she said.

Jack grabbed his refilled cup, thanked Ruth, and left the store.

Bobby joined Ruth behind the counter and readied the insulated cups while Ruth patiently explained to the customers why they couldn't have their gourmet coffee concoctions.

"I'm sorry, but we don't have anything that requires steamed milk or organic tea leaves. We've just got coffee, decaf, and coffee, caf. Oh, and there's cream and sugar, if you like."

A young man was the last in line. He wore a green bandanna and baggy brown trousers that ended before they could provide any warmth to his ankles. A slender braided ponytail snaked down his back. "So I can't get a chai tea here?" A coiled silver ring winked on the finger he used to shove thick glasses farther up his nose.

"No, but you can have a chocolate dipped éclair that will really toot your horn," Ruth suggested.

"Does it have animal products in it?"

"Uh, well, eggs, butter, and milk, among other things. No lard, right, honey?"

Monk nodded at her over his steaming pot of what would become soup.

"Are the eggs from free-range chickens?"

"They're from Tookie Newman's farm," Monk called out. "They've got a chicken coop, but most of the time he just chases them all over creation when they squeeze through the fencing. Does that count as free range?"

"Never mind," he said. "I'll just have some hot water and a tea bag," he said. "Here's my mug." He slid a dented tin cup across the counter.

Bobby shot him a raised eyebrow.

"I'm not into polluting the earth with polystyrene," he said.

"Okay," Ruth said as she gingerly filled the cup with hot water while Bobby grabbed a tea bag. "Are you in town for the Fog Festival?"

He counted out a handful of coins. "Sure am. I'm one of the vendors, art and crystals, mostly. My name's Rocky Bippo." Ruth noticed a heavy silver chain looped around his neck under his smock.

"Fantastic," Ruth said, marveling that the festival was attracting exotic people from all over, people who drank chai tea and traveled.

"Have you gone to many festivals this year?"

"Yeah, this is our fifth this season. See ya around." Rocky took his tea and left.

Bobby picked up a box of chocolates lying on the counter behind the cash register. "Afternoon snack?" she asked, smiling.

Ruth chuckled. "Though I have been known to consider chocolate a meal unto itself, this is actually to serve as someone's salary. Have you met Alva Hernandez?"

"No. I don't think so."

"Well, you will, if you stay for any length of time. He's the town newspaper boy. He's helping me exercise my birds the days I'm working a long shift here."

Bobby nodded. "Actually, Uncle Monk told me about the birds. And the worms." She added slyly, "He told me about you, too. I've never heard him sound so happy."

Ruth blushed. "Oh, well, anyway, Alva lives with Mrs. Hodges."

Bobby looked confused. "Why doesn't he live with his parents?"

"His parents? Oh, Alva is eighty-five years old. I forgot to mention he's the only senior citizen newspaper

boy in Finny. He lives with Mrs. Hodges in exchange
for fixing anything electrical. He's a genius that way. His
family used to own the Pistol Bang Mushroom Farm."
She restacked a pile of paper napkins. "Alva doesn't
have much use for money, but he has a completely
insatiable sweet tooth. He drives a hard bargain, too.
This week it was a box of soft-centered chocolates, no
nuts, no caramels."

Bobby laughed and looked out the front window.
"Uh, Ruth? I think that might be your bird sitter
running up the sidewalk right now."

Sure enough, Alva was racing along the walkway
holding on to his baseball cap, with a cluster of honking
birds at his heels.

"Incoming!" he shouted as the swarm of birds
overtook him, careening in round-eyed terror to escape
two dogs slobbering on their flippered heels.

Running along behind them was a gangly woman
holding their unattached leashes in one hand and
desperately trying to grab the slowest dog's collar
with the other. "Stop, Maxie!" she panted, frantically
shaking strands of silvering hair out of her face.

Bobby and Ruth ran out of Monk's Coffee and
Catering trailing behind the leash lady, looking, Ruth
imagined, like the parade of characters from some
Brothers Grimm fable.

They all came to a confused stop at the fenced back
lot of Luis Puzan's grocery store. All of the birds except
Rutherford managed to squeeze under the chain link
fence, leaving their feathered companion attempting
to squeeze his wide bottom underneath the rail to join
them.

Alva clung to the fence about three feet above the sidewalk, looking down anxiously on the two dogs that growled below him. His denim-covered seat hovered a fraction above the dental range of the snarling animals.

The lady stopped. She spoke in hushed tones to the dogs. Deftly she clipped the leash onto the wiry-haired one and edged her way toward the enormous white dog who was inching up to Rutherford, teeth bared.

Ruth reached out to stop the dog, fearing that Rutherford would have a complete cardiac incident any second.

"Stop!" the woman hissed. "Don't touch him." Her pale eyes glittered with unguarded emotion.

Ruth backed up.

The woman continued to talk soothingly to the dog. She touched him gently on the rear end and worked her way upward until she snapped the leash on his collar. The huge creature turned to face the woman and buried his bony head between her knees, whimpering.

"I'm sorry," the woman said, straightening and turning to Ruth. "I didn't mean to yell at you. Peanut has been through a lot, and he has to be handled carefully. I was just getting them out of their crate when the birds went by, and they took off before I could leash them."

Ruth nodded, her heart still pounding. She picked Rutherford up and handed him to Bobby. "Alva, are you okay? I think you can come down now."

The man grinned and hunkered down from the fence. "What a thing. I haven't moved that fast since old Pauley's bull took a liking to me."

She helped him climb down from the fence. "I am Ruth, and this is Alva Hernandez and Bobby Walker. Alva was walking my birds for me. None of them can fly, so they have to have their daily gadabout."

"I'm Evelyn Bippo. I'm with the Dog House group. We're showing our adoptable dogs at the Fog Festival." There was a faded Dog House logo on the front of her stained sweatshirt.

"Bippo? I think we just met another Bippo," Bobby added.

"Rocky? He's my brother; he's a vendor. Actually, we just finished the Sand and Surf festival down south. There are three or four of the vendors that travel together year-round. I'm always looking for a gathering to show the dogs, so I go to as many as I can."

Bobby looked at the dog, who continued to cower between Evelyn's legs. "What's his story?"

Evelyn shook her head. "Peanut is a wonderful, gentle dog," she said, a sharp edge in her voice. "He was adopted by a terrible jerk who tried to make him a guard dog by beating and starving him. Now he's completely broken, and he only listens to me."

Bobby's eyes filled with anger. "That's awful."

"Yes, it is. Just look at his ears." She widened her legs slightly so they could see the pink stumpy edges where the ears should have been. "The awful man thought since Peanut is part pit bull, he would look fiercer with cropped ears. Whoever did it nearly chopped them off."

Ruth felt sickened.

"I'm sorry," Evelyn said. "I am really not the militant type, but I just can't believe someone could do that to a gentle boy like Peanut."

She scratched her nose with a long, calloused finger. "Anyway, I am really sorry my dogs gave you a fright." She nodded apologetically to Alva. "And are your birds okay?" she asked Ruth.

"They seem to be fine, just winded." Rutherford had recovered enough to poke through Bobby's apron pockets.

"Okay. Well, I'd better get these guys back to camp. It was nice to meet you. I'll see you again, I'm sure."

They watched Evelyn gently lead the dogs away. Peanut stayed so close to her leg that she stumbled every few feet.

"Well, sweet cheeks," Alva said to Ruth, "I'm afraid this adventure is gonna cost you. Next week, I'm raising my fees to fudge."

Ruth stopped on her way to Royland's, the package of worm castings tucked under one arm and a bucket of her finest wigglers clasped in her cold fingers. The empty lot where Ed Honeysill died was quiet in the predusk. The hot air balloons were packed away except for the one taken as evidence. The rest had vanished along with the fog. In their place was a towering stack of Coastal Comets in street clothes, practicing for their performance that would commence in the morning.

Canvas-covered booths lined the rectangular field, sporting signs advertising various culinary delights, from fried artichoke hearts to falafel. The scent of popcorn lingered in the air. It seemed incomprehensible that a man had plunged to his death in that very field. A few stragglers were milling about, bags clutched in their hands, and there was still a line at the baked potato booth.

Ruth plodded along past the swaying tower of Coastal Comets until she noticed Maude in the far corner of the field, banging hard on a black metal box.

Alva stood next to the woman, a purple container in his hands. "Yer just going to bust it," he said.

"Give me the fog juice, you old geezer," Maude snapped.

Ruth approached reluctantly. "What in the world are you two up to?"

"Hi, Ruth," Alva said as he wiped his nose with a piece of fabric that looked suspiciously like a necktie. "I was on my way to the bakery to see if they got any leftovers when this nutzo started banging on that thing. She's going to bust it."

"What is it?" Ruth asked before Maude could explode.

"It's a fog machine, for your information. I've just got to put in the juice and it will work perfectly. I'm testing it out for tomorrow."

"A fog machine?" Ruth was incredulous. "Maude, why do we need a fog machine? This is Finny, remember?"

"Our naturally occurring variety is a little sparse, if

you haven't noticed. The rotten stuff has been thick as pea soup the entire week, and now it has deserted us in our hour of need. I want to make sure this thing works. It will enhance the atmosphere," she said, pouring liquid into a spout. "Where are you going? The crowds might pick up any minute now."

"I think it's pretty much done for the day, Maude, but in any case I've just got to run a quick errand. I'll be around if you need me." Ruth watched in wonder as Maude connected the machine to an extension cord and pressed the button.

Nothing happened.

Maude rattled the cord.

Still nothing.

Grumbling, she knelt down in front of the black box and pressed again.

A burst of white smoke fired out of the machine, and Maude fell over backward, her skirt flying over her head and baring her Vanity Fairs for all the Coastal Comets to see.

The most airborne of the Comets laughed so vigorously that he slipped, causing a domino effect until all eight of them landed in the soft dirt.

Alva roared with glee as he trotted away.

Ruth saw the wisdom in a hasty getaway, as well, once she saw that Maude was not hurt, and she continued on her way to Royland's farm.

As she walked onto his property, it saddened her to see the sign indicating that a portion of Royland's beloved farm was for sale. She knew it killed him to part with even an inch of his land, but it had become too much for one man and an unenthusiastic son to manage. Royland was one of her best customers. She supplied him five buckets of worm castings a month to enrich the soils on his farm.

Ruth easily could have had one of the local teens run the bucket of worms and castings up to Royland's place. They would do anything for pocket money. But the trip was a way to escape the chaos of the festival and a means to delay her inevitably uncomfortable conversation with Candace. She walked past cottages and small fenced pastures, a small white bucket in each hand, trying to think of ways to break her news to the woman.

She arrived at her first stop to find a gaggle of young adults seated on a rickety picnic bench in front of Lemmon's Organic Greens. At harvesttime Royland hired extra help to handpick his precious crop of arugula, spinach, and endive. She recognized Bert Penny and a few of his compatriots from the junior college, and Lizzie Putney, a twenty-year-old local girl whom Ruth had known for years. They were enthusiastically discussing the recent murder.

"Oh man," Bert said. "I heard it was gruesome. The guy fell out of the basket and hung from the edge, all screaming and everything, until he fell. Splat!"

"Gross, Bert," said Lizzie. "Did you actually see it?"

"Nah, I was helping with the parking," he said. "But I heard all about it from Dan."

"Hi, Mrs. Budge," Lizzie called, jumping up to give her a hug. "What brings you here?"

"I'll be busy at the festival tomorrow, so I have

to get my errands done today. I see you all have been putting in a hard day's work." She motioned to their hands, stained green from nails to knuckles.

"Yeah," said Bert. "But Mr. Lemmon pays us okay, and we get dinner, too."

"Sounds like a good deal to me."

Royland and Hugh approached carrying shallow wooden crates. Royland greeted her warmly, putting down his load to take the two buckets from her hands. His voice was lightly peppered with an Argentinean accent.

"My supplies. Wonderful. I'm working on something new. Come and see."

He led the way to a greenhouse filled with tiny seedlings in peat pots and complex networks of irrigation tubing. On a workbench nearby was an empty basket and piles of loamy soil. She breathed in the wonderful scent of well-tended earth.

"I'm going to try hanging herb baskets. Thought the city folks might be interested in something they could keep in a small patio area. I was thinking thyme, maybe some arugula, and chervil. I want to make sure the whole thing is organic. You think your worms are up to the challenge?"

"I think they'll help your pots out tremendously as long as you don't overwater them."

"No problem. Easy on the water."

They left the humid space and walked back outside. Nestled next to the greenhouse was a split-rail pen containing a gargantuan, spotted pig.

"Hello, Noodles," she called out.

The pig dashed excitedly to the fence to sniff her hand. About six inches away from the fence line, she stopped, cocked her head, and wheeled around in retreat.

"I know. You thought Phillip was with me, didn't you? When are you going to stop looking for him?"

Ruth had the sudden realization that she had stopped thinking about Phillip every day. When had that happened? It had come so gradually she hadn't noticed. She felt a strange pang of guilt, but it vanished quickly. Thoughts of Phillip did not crowd her mind, because she was busy with her life with Monk. One did not replace the other, she thought with wonder. Both men occupied different places in her psyche. *Our God is an awesome God,* she thought.

Ruth and Royland chatted for a bit about the recent events as they walked.

"My helpers are having a tough time keeping their mind on their work. All this talk about the murder."

They watched the group on the picnic bench. Hugh stood apart from the rest, fiddling with some tubing. "I wish he'd try a little harder to fit in," Royland said. "I think that Lizzie would treat him okay if he would just talk to her. He's just not much for social things."

Ruth nodded, thinking that Hugh looked mighty comfortable clanking around Pistol Bang's. "Maybe he hasn't found the right girl yet." Apparently Hugh's father had no idea his son had developed quite a relationship with Dimple.

"At twenty-two I don't know what he's waiting for," he said, retrieving his crate. "I was married by then and working toward buying my place here."

"I think it was an accident, someone shooting as a joke or something," Lizzie was saying. "What do you think, Hugh?"

"Oh, I dunno." Ruth saw him duck his head.

"Did you see it happen, Hugh?" Bert asked, eagerness painted all over his face.

"I saw the balloon crash, but I didn't see the guy fall out," Hugh said.

Bert sighed with disappointment. "Bummer."

"Okay, you slackers," Royland announced, "back to work."

Yes, Ruth thought, there's no more avoiding it. Time to visit the grieving widow.

―

A short while later, Ruth was just about to tap on the door of room number 7 when she heard voices from inside.

"Look, I know it's been rough on you, but you're free now."

"How can you do this to me?" Candace's voice cracked. "He's dead, for pity's sake."

"You didn't love him, Candace. It's not like you lost the great love of your life. Just cut the sentimental routine. You can do what you want now. We can be together."

"It's not that easy, Bing."

"It's exactly that easy. Your husband is dead. Time to move on."

"Get out!"

"Okay, hon," Bing said, "but think about it. It's a win/win. We were made for each other. You know we could have the time of our lives."

At that moment, the door swung open,. and Ruth was wishing she had thought to retreat when she first realized whom she was overhearing. Bing did not seem at all nonplussed to find Ruth on the other side. "Hello, Mrs. Budge." He showed a dazzling white smile. "See you later."

Candace came to the door in a pink satin robe and slippers. Her face was gaunt.

"Hello, Candace. I'm terribly sorry to intrude right now, but I need to talk to you about something." She hesitated. "I didn't mean to interrupt your conversation with Bing."

"Don't worry about it. He was just leaving anyway."

"Is everything okay? I couldn't help but overhear—," she prodded. She wondered what Candace must be feeling, knowing that she betrayed her adoring husband before he was murdered.

"There's nothing between us two." She walked to the window. "I can't believe I ever saw anything in him. I must have been insane." She pressed her fingers to the glass.

"How did you meet?"

"I met him in Oregon, at some festival that Ed dragged me to. Bing is a spoiled, egocentric child. If anyone tells him no, all he hears is 'Keep asking until it's yes.' His parents sent him off to boarding school after he drove his motorcycle through a flower shop window. I guess it was easier than actually attempting to discipline him. Anyway, we were attracted to each other at the beginning, but then I saw him for what he was. I kept away for a long time." Her voice trailed off. "Not long enough, though."

Ruth sat still on the sofa, afraid to startle Candace away from her narrative.

"It happened after I lost the baby," Candace continued. "I got pregnant, and Ed was so excited. Then I miscarried early on. Ed was devastated, but he was more worried about me. He smothered me, hovering over me every moment. I couldn't stand it. He was driving me nuts with all his mothering. I just wanted to get away from him, and everything." She stopped talking and closed her eyes. "Bing is gorgeous, spontaneous, exciting. Everything my husband wasn't."

Ruth looked around the small room, buying time. She noticed a neat row of nail polish bottles on the coffee table. Electric blue, turquoise. Shell pink. It made her shudder.

"I am so sorry about your husband. I know how hard it is to lose a spouse."

"You do?" she said, turning. "Thank you. This feels like a nightmare. I'm really tired. What did you want to talk to me about?"

"I need to talk to Detective Denny about the— accident. He wants to ask me a few more questions."

Candace stared at her. "Uh-huh."

"I, er, I need to tell him the truth about everything. He's a good officer and a personal friend, like a son, actually."

"Okay. Why did you need to tell me that?"

Ruth felt the words burning in her mouth. "I know you were with Bing Mitchell just before the accident. Did you tell the police about that?"

Candace stared long enough that Ruth feared she didn't hear the question.

"You know? How do you know?" she whispered.

"Let's just say I was in the vicinity and I, er, overheard some things. I wanted you to know that I have to tell the detective. I certainly don't want to cause you any embarrassment, but he needs to know. I'm sure he will be discreet."

"Why?" Candace's pitch rose nearly an octave. "Why does he have to be told?"

"Because he needs to figure out who may have had a motive to kill your husband."

The young woman's lips moved, but no words came out.

"Candace, it's possible that after your argument with Bing, he shot the flare at the balloon himself."

"Why on earth would he do that?"

"He was jealous of your husband? He's in love with you, maybe?"

"Bing never loved me, not like Ed did."

But he seems intent on possessing you, Ruth thought. "I heard some talk. That Bing was supposed to go up with Ed in the balloon but he was late, so one of his people went up instead." She looked at Candace's stark face. "I'm really so sorry. Please forgive me for causing you any more pain." She glanced at her watch. "I'd better go now." She rose to leave.

Candace wrinkled her brows and pressed a ragged fingernail against her lips. "I can't believe this. Nothing like this should have happened to him."

"Did Ed ever get into any trouble?"

"Trouble? I don't think so. He had some financial strain when we first got married. Then things seemed to even out. Do you think someone had a grudge against him?" she asked, blinking through tears.

"I don't know. I'm not sure what to think."

"I will talk to the police, tell them what happened."

"I think that would be best. Good-bye, Candace."

As Ruth walked down the quiet hallway, she was struck by an awful thought. Candace had insinuated that she was bored with her life with Ed. She felt the union was forced on her by her father.

If Bing wanted to, he had plenty of time after his assignation to fire a shot at Ed Honeysill's balloon.

But so, too, did Candace.

6

The morning church service was subdued. The pastor spoke about death as a new beginning. Ruth knew it was true, that this life was only a stopover on a journey to a much better place with God. But all the same, she wondered what He thought about it all. How did He feel when His precious gift of life was taken away before it was meant to be?

In her mind it was a terrible thing to disrespect a divine gift in such a brutal, callous way. For some reason, Pickles Peckenpaugh surfaced in her mind. She thought about the journal, the fantastic characters who were once flesh and blood and now faded to memories. Hopefully she would have time later to read more about their escapades.

After church she kissed Monk good-bye and shouldered her camera bag on her way to a fenced area in the middle of the festival grounds. Ruth thought it looked much like a canine United Nations convention as she wandered around the fence line taking pictures to appease her ferocious publicity chairwoman. She was not sure if she had the patience to put up with Maude for one day plus another whole weekend of Festival activities, but she was determined to try.

The large penned area housed five smaller pens with yelping, napping, panting, and sniffing doggy delegates. A litter of wiry terrier puppies were jumbled together in a collective nap, gushed over by a pair of heart-warmed humans.

"Oh, Jeff. Aren't they adorable?" the young woman said, holding her long hair out of her face as she bent over the enclosure. Jeff agreed aloud that they were definitely precious.

Ruth saw Evelyn Bippo, the lady who had saved Alva from her enthusiastic dogs, hurry over to talk to them about the rigors of puppy adoption. The huge, earless white dog—Peanut, Ruth recalled—followed immediately behind her. Evelyn told them of the fees involved, mandatory obedience training, and the various annoying stages of dog maturation ranging from indoor accidents to the occasional dog neurosis that can result in the animal chewing the siding off the house.

Ruth listened intently. Birds and worms she knew about, but dogs were not in her menagerie.

She glanced to the left and saw Rocky Bippo, Evelyn's chai tea-loving brother, watching from outside the enclosure, his elbows resting on the fence just above a banner reading THE DOG HOUSE. He nodded at her. Gesturing to the young couple, he said, "They're going home with a puppy. I've seen that look many times before, and no amount of warnings will make a dent."

"Your sister works hard for those dogs, doesn't she?"

He nodded, and a tiny silver moon sparkled in his earlobe. "Yeah, she feels more in tune with animals than people sometimes. We both do, but she's a softy for anything with whiskers."

Evelyn walked with the couple to the exit, smiling as they left. Then she came over to Rocky, nodding to Ruth.

"They're going to buy a leash and dog bed." Evelyn

beamed. "That's the second adoption today."

"Great, Ev. Anyone for the older guys?"

Her smile faded as she contemplated the cages on the far side of the gated oval. "No. You know how it goes with the older ones." She reached down to stroke the neck of the earless giant with his head between her legs. "What will happen to our friends, Peanut?" The lines on her forehead deepened.

"Maybe things will look up. We've got two more days of festival to go next weekend."

Ruth moved away to take pictures of the Dog House banner, but she remained close enough to hear Evelyn and her brother.

Evelyn stroked the dog in her arms absently. "There was a guy here earlier," she said to Rocky in a whisper loud enough for Ruth's eavesdropping. "A rough-looking sort. He was asking me about Cliffy." She pointed to a muscular spotted dog that looked as though it had started out to be a shepherd until its genes reconsidered. "I didn't like the looks of him. I told him he was taken already." She bit her lip nervously. "I know it's getting really expensive to keep them all, but I just couldn't risk it."

"I know. Don't worry about it. We've been through a bad patch, but it's going to be better now. When the festival wraps, we'll take care of our business and be gone before anyone is the wiser."

"You know, I didn't think *he* would be here," Evelyn breathed.

"You're bound to run into him every so often. It's okay—he'll stay away. And if he doesn't, I'll get rid of him." There was an undertone of menace in his voice.

"Pretty tough talk."

He touched her shoulder gently. "You know I mean it, sis."

Ruth looked at the tight line of his lips and the glitter behind his dark eyes. She shivered.

"Yes, I do," the woman said.

An hour later, after stopping at Puzan's for a life-sustaining chocolate bar, Ruth headed for home thinking about Rocky and Evelyn. They were very close. Whom was he talking about getting rid of? And what was the "business" he referred to? There was certainly a lot of tension circling the pair.

The gravel crunched under Ruth's feet. She had turned down the wooded pathway that was a shortcut from the open field upslope to the residential area clustered along the nostrils of Finny's Nose. The air was musky, spiced with azalea and cedar. Afternoon sun penetrated the canopy of branches here and there, dappling the wooded path with streaks of light.

She looked up, admiring the play of sun and shadow farther upslope. There was a sudden glint, a harsh reflected light from the top of Finny's Nose, as if someone was watching the festival below through binoculars. Now who would be doing that?

Ruth felt a prickle of fear on the back of her neck. She quickened her pace and made a beeline for home.

Unfortunately, Maude was standing on her

doorstep when she arrived. "You've got to fix this," she commanded, thrusting a stack of papers out in front of her. "Just look at these flyers. That Len Brewster at the print shop is an idiot."

Ruth scanned the paper advertising the Fig Festival. "Well, Bubby Dean has a pretty robust fig tree on his property."

"This is no time for levity. You've got to go and have them reprinted. They need to be ready for the distribution team."

The team consisted of Flo who was already heavily burdened with managing the bake sale and manning the information booth. "Okay," Ruth said with a sigh. "I'll go talk to Len."

She didn't add, "As soon as I eat lunch."

Len proved to be fairly agreeable about changing the focus of the festival from figs to fog, once he had ascertained that Maude had not accompanied her. Even with his cheerful cooperation, it took an hour plus to make the changes and reprint the flyers.

She heard the ominous sound of the phone ringing when she finally heaved her body home again. "It's okay, Ruth," she said to herself. "Maybe it's a telemarketer."

"Ruth? It's Maude."

Her heart sank. "The flyers are fixed," she said. "Len said there was no charge as long as you stay out of his shop."

"Good. Now you need to bake a dozen treats of some sort. Something sweet that fits in with the fog theme. I'll pick them up tomorrow morning on my way to headquarters."

"The bake sale isn't until the last day of the festival. Why do I need to bake treats now?" She could not keep a whiny edge out of her voice.

"The tasting committee meets tomorrow to decide on the final choices for the bake sale next weekend. We need a variety of treats represented."

"And what are you baking?"

"My famous Cloudy Cashew Chewies."

Maude's Cashew Chewies were indeed famous. They made their debut at the Christmas cookie exchange. No fat, no sugar, and quite definitely no taste whatsoever. "All right," Ruth said heavily. "What am I supposed to bake?"

"Whatever you want. Just make sure it's sweet, doesn't require utensils, will keep well unrefrigerated, and fits the fog theme." Maude hung up.

Ruth slammed the phone down. "That woman has got to have some fascist relatives somewhere in her family tree." It would have been easy to call down to Monk's shop and ask him to rustle up a treat. He would be happy to do it, but she didn't want to add to his heavy workload. She scanned her cupboards, looking for inspiration. Chocolate chips, flour, sugar, espresso powder. Aha! Chocolate chip espresso muffins!

After the muffins were happily packed into the oven, she plopped down on the sofa with the journal.

August the 12th, 1923
Dan was here again tonight. They call him
Soapy Dan because he always comes in clean
and smelling of spice. I think he has his eye on

one of my new dancing girls. I know he didn't come for the hash as he hardly touched a bite.

August the 16th

Slats came today to give us a once-over. We are to expect a group of his friends later on in the month. He wants them to get the royal treatment. The girls came to the dining room to meet him, dressed in their best and looking well. Except for Hazel. If I haven't told her a thousand times to lay off the chocolates! And to boot, she wore that robe de style in a luminous green which made her resemble nothing so much as an acorn squash! Far too plump to be on stage with the others.

I could tell from the way his bushy eyebrows came together that Hazel wasn't going to meet the mark. Sure enough, Slats said the girls were fine but Hazel had to go. But how could the Pickle Jar survive without Hazel? She's been here since we started. In a bit of daring, I told Slats she was the best cook this side of the Rockies and we needed her in the kitchen for those nights when we were to feed his associates. He was doubtful, but he is a businessman first, gangster second. He agreed to keep her on, for cooking duty only.

Fortunately he liked our new Janey. She is a wonderful dancer, I must admit. The customers love to watch her as they eat.

Hazel (along with Bertha, our real

*chef) made a chicken-fried steak and mashed
potatoes. I was impressed. Slats gave his full
approval to the fare. He even tried a few of the
greens, though things of the vegetable persuasion
are against his ways. Even I have to admit the
rhubarb compote was a marvel.*

*He fell asleep in a chair by the fire. He
looked kind of boyish, with his dark patch of
hair thrown over his eyes. I'm not fooled by that
little-boy-lost look. I know he'd murder us all
if he thought we double-crossed him. I shudder
just to think about it. I long for the day when
I can buy the Pickle Jar outright and am no
longer beholden to this man. Soon, maybe next
spring, it will be mine to do with as I please.*

*In spite of the fires which we keep burning
constantly, a cursed fog has settled over our town
like a layer of poisonous fumes. I am worried
more than ever about what will happen when
Slats finds out who stole his bag of cash. I fear
what will come of it, something awful. There
are many desperate people in town who would
do anything to feed their little ones. I just hope
whoever did it runs far away from this gloomy
place. I am not certain, though, if anywhere is
far enough to escape Slats, even in this cloud of
darkness.*

*Only time will tell what wickedness is
buried in this evil fog.*

The kitchen timer startled Ruth. She put the

muffins on a rack to cool and piled the dishes on the counter. The clock chimed—9:30 p.m. and there were still critters to be tended to. It was Monk's late night, and he wouldn't be home for another half hour.

She grabbed a bag of Cheerios and protein pellets and headed out to the yard. After making sure the worm bins were covered, she made her way to the far corner of the grassy space.

"Dinner," she yelled to the undulating swarm of gulls. They followed her to the pen, pushing and pecking at each other. She threw in handfuls of food, and the birds fought their way into the enclosure. Not the sharpest crayons in the box but cooperative where food was concerned. She closed the gate and took one last look into the pen. In the corner, Franklin rested on his bottom. He was missing an eye and a foot after he got tangled in a fishing line and mauled by a dog. The red pucker where his eyeball used to be and the dark gray feathers on his white back gave him the look of a depressed, feathery Eeyore. She generally took Franklin for a hobble along the beach by himself, as it was too hard for him to keep up with the rest of the flock. He looked mournfully up at her.

"Oh, Franklin. I know I promised to take you to the beach, but it's late and I've got a headache."

The bird cocked his head.

"I'm so tired," she said. "I'll take you tomorrow."

He bowed his neck. If he had lips, she swore they would be trembling.

"Good grief," she said as she lifted him up. "How can you lay a guilt trip on me when you can't even talk?" The bird snuggled his satiny head under her chin as she retrieved the slim plastic tube the veterinarian had made to protect his stump of a leg.

"Let's go, Franklin. There are miles to go before we sleep."

———

The beach was dreamlike. The almost-full moon painted the fog in silvery tones and the gravel in tints of ebony and charcoal. It looked like an old black-and-white photograph. She walked along behind Franklin. Waves scurried back and forth to grab handfuls of loose stones, and the air was heavy with moisture and the scent of brine.

The cold was good for her husband's business. People lined up to purchase vats of his clam chowder on days like this. She smiled when she thought of him. They had only been married for six months. She had been married for twenty-five years the time before, until a heart attack stole her husband away. Their life as husband and wife was still so new, so uncertain, but by the grace of God, she was enjoying every minute.

At the moment, though, Ruth was far from enjoying things. Her indigestion was back, perhaps courtesy of her chocolate bar lunch, and a headache pounded the back of her eyes as she trudged along. Her thoughts were scattered, swirling around like the fog that seeped over the hillside to bury Finny once again. One image came to the forefront. Meg Sooner.

Dimple's mother was back, all right, and presumably assuming her role of beloved grandmother.

No one had seen hide nor hair of the woman for twenty years and then she blows into town like Mary Poppins. No, more like Glinda, Ruth thought with hostility. Meg was a delicate woman, well tailored and graceful to boot. Even her voice sounded tinkly and sweet when Ruth had spoken to her on the phone while trying to reach Dimple.

Ruth felt her stomach clenched as she recalled that Dimple confessed to speaking with Meg several times in the past few months. From what she'd gathered, it was a near-fatal car accident that galvanized Meg into reconnecting with her estranged daughter. It stung a bit to know that Dimple had been in contact with her mother and Ruth had not known. Somehow it felt like a betrayal. She wasn't sure why. She was still Cootchie's Nana. Their lives were inevitably intertwined since the day Dimple had asked her to help her through the pregnancy. A biological grandmother couldn't change that.

Could she?

A twist of uncertainty filled her heart.

She wished fervently that Grandma Meg would not be there for the birthday celebration. Ruth's agitated breaths fogged the cold air. Enough about Meg.

Ruth looked up at the moon and thought about the namesake of the town. In this ethereal moment, it was easy to believe that decades ago rumrunners like Frederick Finny would anchor in the choppy water and use smaller boats to ferry their precious Canadian whiskey to shore. It was a simple plan that worked like a charm.

Franklin stumped ahead and vanished around an outcropping of slimy rocks. Ruth hurried to catch up.

Rounding the corner, she stopped abruptly.

It wasn't gangsters waiting on the beach this night.

Three small bonfires burned brightly. Around them sat three figures, clothed in black with hoods up or bandannas tied around their heads. In the center of the group was a woman.

They stopped their talking and leaped up to face Ruth.

Ruth remembered Alva's warning about the proc tologists in search of a sacrificial victim. Her breath froze in her lungs. She could not make out their faces, only the glitter of narrowed eyes. They did not speak, but the biggest one took a step toward her.

"Uh," she began, her heart hammering with the force of a pneumatic drill. "Uh, well. I see you've found the beach."

The big man took another step and reached inside his vest.

"Uh, what a—a lovely night for a bonfire." Ruth's voice trembled.

Now all three figures began to move slowly in Ruth's direction.

"I'll just run and get some marshmallows!" she shrieked. Ruth scooped up Franklin and ran as fast as her middle-aged legs would carry her, reciting the Lord's Prayer all the way home.

Monk immediately began to rifle through the closet when she told him.

"What are you doing?"

He didn't answer her. Finally, he whirled around with a bat in his hand. "I'm going to go down there and teach those young punks a lesson."

"You can't do that," she gasped. "They might be some sort of gang. I called Jack before I got home, and he said he'd go right over and check it out."

"I don't care if they're Attila the Hun's army; they got no right to scare you like that."

It took several minutes of cajoling and pleading to dissuade him from his plan. "Please, honey. They didn't hurt me. They didn't even say a word."

Finally, he reluctantly agreed to suspend his baseball bat mission. They lay down to sleep, but several hours later her eyes were still wide open. She went downstairs and booted up the computer, typing in "ecoterrorists."

The deluge of information surprised her.

Millions of dollars of property damage. Intimidation. Harassment. Arson.

So there really were cells of people who orchestrated attacks against ranchers, loggers, miners, the government, et cetera.

Maybe Alva was right. Maybe the green bandanna folks were planning to carry out some action in Finny.

One line in the news article she was reading jumped out.

"One group even distributes manuals on how to infiltrate a target area and escape without being caught."

With cold fingers, she turned off the computer.

7

"You must be Detective Denny," Meg said to Jack. "It's so good to see you." She looked poised and calm in her green sweater set and slacks. "We're so glad you could come for dinner, even if you have to cook it."

"Hello. We're glad to be here. Mondays are usually quiet around the office, but today has been nuts. It's good to get out of there for a while." He handed her a bowl of potato salad. "We're in luck. Louella made this, which saves everyone from having to eat mine."

She laughed and took the bowl. "Is this your son?" she asked, trying to see around Jack's leg to the boy who clung there, his head under his father's flannel shirt.

"Yes, this is Paul. Can you say hello, Paul?" Jack patted the boy's head through the fabric. "He isn't much of a conversationalist."

"No problem. Cootchie is in the backyard, I think."

They excused themselves and headed outside.

Dimple greeted him with a hug.

In no time Cootchie and Paul were busy digging a hole. Dimple set Jack to work firing up the barbecue and handed him a platter of something.

He looked up from his study of the foodstuffs as Ruth joined him. "Hey, Ruth." He lowered his voice and looked suspiciously at the slender brown cylinders on the grill. "What in the world is a meatless hot dog made out of anyway?"

"Probably the same thing the cake frosting is made out of. In my experience, it's best just to go with the flow and not ask too many questions."

He laughed and wiped his long fingers on a KISS THE COOK apron. "I think you're right. Where's your hubby tonight?"

"He's got a catering gig in Half Moon Bay."

"You look tired," he said as he slid the food onto the grill.

"I couldn't sleep last night. I tried to nap today, but Maude has always got me doing something or other. I spent the entire morning and early afternoon bagging beads to use at the craft table. Do you think we can expect two hundred kids to attend next weekend?"

He laughed. "Not unless Disneyland suddenly packs up and moves here." He glanced back at the kitchen. "I wonder if Meg is enjoying her stay." He could see a question in Ruth's eyes. The same question that was no doubt hovering in the back of his own. Why had Meg Sooner come back to Finny? Neither had a chance to vocalize their thoughts, as Meg and Dimple emerged, carrying presents to the lighted patio.

"Cootchie," Dimple called. "Why don't you open your presents before Mr. Denny has our dinner ready?"

They all gathered around the birthday girl, and Paul helped Cootchie open the gifts.

The girl squealed at the set of magnifying glasses from Jack and Paul and the fossil excavation kit from Ruth. Everyone leaned forward a little closer to see Cootchie unwrap the glittering package from Meg Sooner. It was a porcelain doll, dressed in pink velvet with delicate orange curls and painted eyelashes. The doll was gorgeous and expensive.

Jack saw the tiny gleam of satisfaction on Ruth's face when Cootchie tossed the doll onto the grass and hauled Paul away to start an archaeological dig.

"Oh dear. I thought all girls liked dolls," Meg said.

"I'm sure she'll love playing dolls after she gets the digging out of her system," Ruth said.

"Maybe you're right. I think I've got a lot to learn about my granddaughter. And my daughter." Meg looked at Dimple as she gathered up the crumpled paper.

After potato salad and meatless hot dogs smothered in organic mustard, Dimple and Meg set to work on the dishes. Jack and Ruth walked outside to watch the children digging by porch light in the yard. The sky was heavy with a wet blanket of fog. Pockets of brilliant star-speckled velvet poked through here and there. The round moon escaped its foggy mantle from time to time to bathe the yard in white light.

"Have you come to any conclusions about Ed's death?" Ruth asked.

"Only that we don't know who did it. There are so many people in town right now." He had one visitor pulling his mind away from work matters. The tiny dark-haired woman who had turned out to be Monk's niece. "So, er, is Bobby finding time to enjoy the festival?"

Ruth nodded. "Yes, but I think she would like Finny better without the crowds. She is always out on a hike or a run. She seems to thrive in the chill."

He wanted to ask how long Bobby was going to stay, but he couldn't think of a graceful way to do so.

After a while, the group assembled again on the porch to choke down carrot cake with tofu frosting. Even Meg seemed to require a lot of iced tea to get the stuff headed in the right direction.

Cootchie put down her paper plate and threw her head back to look at the sky. "It's de worm moon," she said, pointing upward.

"The what, dear?" Meg leaned down.

"She said it's the worm moon," Dimple repeated.

They all looked up at the almost full moon, outlined by a frame of ghostly fog.

"What does that mean, exactly?" Meg asked, her brow wrinkled.

"It's a Native American name to describe the full moon that occurs in March. As the temperature begins to warm, earthworm casts appear, trumpeting the return of the robins."

"Nana has worms," Cootchie said. She hugged Ruth around the knees. "She has a worm farm."

"Oh boy. I'm sure your, er, Mrs. Sooner doesn't want to hear about that."

"About what? I'd love to know more about you. You've been so good to my granddaughter."

Ruth was saved from having to answer when an explosion lit the sky with a bright orange fireball. The partygoers all stood openmouthed for a moment.

Jack reacted first. "Dimple, can you keep Paul here for a while? I've gotta go."

Dimple and Meg ushered the two children into the house. Ruth jogged along behind him. "Can I come with you?" she asked.

He hesitated only a moment. "Sure. I take it fire and catastrophe are preferable to the present awkward situation?"

"Exactly."

As they roared down the rock walkway and onto the main road, the dispatcher filled Jack in on the location of the explosion. He radioed for a fire engine as gravel shot out from under the speeding tires.

Jack enjoyed the frantic drive to the makeshift trailer park, all the while being careful of his passenger. Sometimes driving code three was the only perk of the job.

They arrived to find a fire blazing and people either running or clumped together in shocked groups. Jack made Ruth promise to stay out of the way of anything flaming and strode off toward the chaos.

The small trailer was burning fiercely, the flames licking at the striped awning. The interior was a swirl of fire and heavy smoke, punctuated by loud cracks and whooshing noises. A man in baggy clothes with a bandanna wrapped around his head squirted a lackluster stream of foam on the blaze with a fire extinguisher.

Seconds later a woman ran up to the trailer. She clutched a quilted robe around her tall frame. "Oh no, Rocky. Your trailer. Is anyone inside? Are you hurt?"

"No," he snarled, continuing to wave the extinguisher in erratic arcs in front of him, wiping at the sweat on his stubbled face. "Go back to your trailer. I'll come and get you when it's over."

Several men ran up to assist Rocky. They all wore green bandannas. The other fair vendors just watched the melee; some drank coffee, one ate a hot dog, and two still clutched their playing cards in front of them.

Jack worked to keep the bystanders back a safe distance from the fire. The trailer door next to him opened. Bing Mitchell stood there wearing a blue sweat suit. His feet were bare, and even his toes looked well muscled. He surveyed the scene with amusement.

"Hey there, Detective. Did you come for the campfire? This town is definitely a hot spot. I just can't get over it." His face glowed oddly in the moonlight. "What is that idiot doing?"

"Which idiot?"

"Rocky Bippo, the idiot with the fire extinguisher. And his sister, the dog lady. She's nuttier than he is. They're into some gang that goes around wreaking havoc on the general population. What is it about those two? Trouble follows them everywhere."

Before Jack could follow up on the strange comments, a fire engine careened into the area and disgorged several young volunteers who leaped off the rig with undisguised exuberance. The two seasoned firefighters exited the vehicle in a more sedate manner. One of them was the chief of the Finny Fire Department, Ernie Gonzalez.

"Hey, Jack," Ernie said as the others donned helmets and unrolled hose. "Nice little bonfire." A lush mustache draped over his plump cheeks. "What do you make of it?"

A deafening blast followed by a rocketing arc of

fire caused them all to duck.

Jack straightened up tentatively. "Propane tank?"

Ernie guffawed. "You're getting good, J.D. Maybe there's hope for you yet. Let's get some wet stuff on the red stuff and we'll debrief in a while." He turned his attention to the blaze. "Now get everybody out of the way," he said over his shoulder.

Jack followed directions as he moved back and persuaded Rocky Bippo to follow him. Ruth hurried over.

"Can you tell me what happened?" Jack pierced Rocky with a steady gaze.

Rocky shook his head. His long hair flowed out of the bottom of his bandanna like an oil slick. "I don't know. I was reading in my trailer, and all of a sudden I heard a sound. Like a hissing or something. I was just opening the front door to check it out when—boom—the trailer tank exploded. Pretty soon the whole side of the trailer was on fire. I grabbed an extinguisher out of the truck and tried to put it out. A couple of the guys ran to get theirs, too, but it was too big by then. Then the other tanks went up."

"Were they your tanks?"

"Yeah. I use them to make the mushrooms."

Jack blinked, nodding to Mary Dirisi as she arrived on the scene.

Rocky tore his gaze from the fire. "I heat up PVC pipe with a propane torch. When it starts to burn, you can shape it and it gets stippled and discolored. Looks just like mushrooms. I sell them as garden art."

"Have you had any problems with the tanks before?"

"No. They're just small handheld jobs. I've never had a lick of trouble." He caught sight of Bing standing with his arms folded watching the blaze. "Never trouble with the tanks, anyway."

Evelyn Bippo was dressed in jeans and a worn T-shirt when she ran up to her brother. "Rocky, I can't find Edmund. I've looked everywhere."

Jack put a hand on his radio. "Who's Edmund?"

Rocky sighed. "Don't worry, Detective. He's a dog. A crazy beagle." He turned to Evelyn. "Is everybody else accounted for?"

She nodded, tears filling her eyes. "Just Edmund. I think the explosions scared him and he jumped over the enclosure." The fingernail she pressed to her lips was bitten to the quick. The firelight accentuated the creases in her forehead and cast eerie shadows on her face.

Rocky hugged her tightly and walked her away to a quiet corner, offering consolation as he went. "It's okay, Ev. We'll find him."

A sweaty Chief Gonzalez approached.

"Hey, Ruth. Those wigglers you got me really did the trick. I caught a ten-pound trout that was a thing of beauty."

"I'm glad, Ernie."

"Me, too. The wife's always on me about spending a whole day catching nothing but a cold." He snorted. "Okay, Jack. Here's the deal. Someone set fire to the stack of newspapers under the trailer's propane tank."

"How do you know?"

"Because I'm a stud," Ernie answered. He held up a half-melted lighter. "And we found this a few yards away in the grass."

With a grin, Jack scribbled notes on a pad. "Uh-huh. That's what set the trailer on fire?"

"Yup. The fire caused the propane to expand until the release valve failed and then—*kablam*." He jerked his meaty thumbs toward the night sky. "That set the smaller tanks off, too."

"Does anybody know where this guy belongs?" Mary stood with a shivering dog cradled in her arms. The animal was panting heavily, leaving rivulets of drool on her pants.

Evelyn appeared at her elbow. "It's Edmund. He's mine." She gently took the dog and inspected him. The worry in her eyes turned to profound relief. "Where did you find him, Officer?"

"I was getting out of my car and he practically knocked me over." She looked fondly at the dog. "He didn't want to come at first, but I persuaded him with some peanut butter crackers I had with me."

"Is he okay, Evelyn?" Ruth asked.

She nodded as she massaged the dog behind his ears. "I think so. Just scared mostly. He's not used to being on his own. I only got him a few months ago."

"She runs a dog adoption service," Ruth said.

"Really?" Mary's eyebrows lifted. "So this guy needs a home?"

Evelyn, Rocky, and Ruth all nodded vigorously. Jack looked on in amusement.

"Maybe it's meant to be. When I'm done here, you can tell me more about Edmund," she said. "I've been thinking I need a dog in my life."

"Come over to my trailer. I've got his history, at least as much as we know."

"I certainly don't want this fire scene to get in the way of a good matchmaking session," Jack said, "but would you mind getting some statements, Mary?"

"Sure thing, boss. I'll come by your trailer later," she said to Evelyn, giving Edmund a final pat.

Rocky lingered behind, his eyes narrowed. He seemed to come to some internal decision. "I'm going to give Ev a hand. I'll be at her trailer if you need me."

Jack nodded as Rocky walked away.

"I'm going to be here awhile, Ruth. Let me arrange a ride for you back to Dimple's. Tell her I'll be by for Paul as soon as I can."

"Okay, though I know Cootchie will be thrilled to tuck him into her trundle bed. Poor kid, he'll be eating soybeans for breakfast."

8

The contestants in the Fog Festival cook-off were serious about their endeavors. Ruth picked up on the vibes even before she began taking pictures of the cooking enthusiasts packed into the courtyard of the Finny Hotel. It was the only weekday event. The dishes would be prepared and judged that evening, and the prizes awarded on the last day of the festival. Ruth thought it ironic that the big payola for first prize was an overnight stay at a bed-and-breakfast in neighboring Half Moon Bay. Second prize was a free ticket to the church spaghetti feed and a new spatula.

Outside of the cooking chaos, a giant white tent trembled in the cool breeze. It had been erected in a vacant lot to accommodate the Fog Festival staff and visitors. A half dozen people bustled back and forth from the tent, staggering under the weight of produce crates. Others sat on picnic benches outside soaking up the newly arrived sunshine. The scent of cypress and woody azalea mingled with aromas of garlic and tangy feta. A slight smell of smoke still hung in the air from the fire the previous evening.

Ruth saw the Sassie sisters, Lena and Anne, huddling in conference over a steaming pot of split pea soup, wearing matching green shirts almost the same color as their entry. Several people Ruth did not know tended their portable ovens and microwaves. A smoked salmon contingent poked at their specimen with all the precision of a neurosurgery team.

Royland Lemmon wheeled a squeaky dolly in front of him. It was so loaded with crates of arugula and radicchio that only his head was visible over the top. Squealing to a stop, he pushed back his worn cowboy hat with a thumb.

"Ruth," he said as his face crumpled into wrinkles. "It's nice to see you." His chipped front tooth lent him a comical look.

"It's nice to see you, too. Are you supplying the greens today?"

"Yes, ma'am. I've got six more crates of goodness in the truck. Fresh picked this morning." His brown eyes shone with pride. "You want a bunch to take with you?"

"I'd love a bunch," she said, taking the greens from his calloused hands. She buried her face in the tender green leaves and inhaled a lungful of spicy contentment. "Monk can make an amazing salad with this."

"My pleasure. I know you both appreciate my greens. Say, have you seen my son around here anywhere? I need him to help me unload these crates." Royland shook his head. "He's always off somewhere."

"He told me about his truffle business. What an interesting idea."

The man shook his head again. "Is that what it is now? Truffles? I thought he was still in the ergonomic bicycle seat racket. It's always something new."

Royland gazed off toward the coastline and sighed. "He's desperate to escape the life I've made here. Ever since his mother divorced me when he was twelve. The kids in school have always been rough on him, too."

His shoulders sagged. "He just can't wait to get away from here. And me."

"I'm sorry, Royland. I do know how it feels." She thought about her own son who had moved to a different state to get away. Then she caught sight of Hugh. "Oh, he's over there, talking to the balloon man, Bing. I'm on my way to that side; I'll tell him you need his help at the truck."

"Thank you, ma'am. You enjoy that arugula now."

"I certainly will." She made her way past the clam chowder team to the two men. They were deep in conversation. Hugh's young face was rapt with interest.

"I'll bet you've been all over. How long have you been in the business?" she heard Hugh ask.

"Forever, it seems like. I know everything there is to know about it." Bing slouched against a freezer. "Ballooning has been around for generations. Many people don't know that the Japanese actually used balloons as makeshift bombs to terrorize our mainland during the war."

"No way." Hugh stared at his companion.

"It's absolutely true. They called them Fugo balloons." Bing scanned the crowd as he talked. "The Japs made crude balloons, just rubberized silk envelopes really, and filled them with hydrogen. They launched them into the Gulf Stream and let the air currents take them across the Pacific to the United States."

"Awesome. Did any of them make it?"

"Not many. Most didn't survive the weather. The Fugos only killed one person, a woman picnicking with her kids in Maryland."

"Unbelievable," Hugh said, his Adam's apple bobbing excitedly. "All that work and it didn't even make a difference."

It made quite a difference to the woman in Maryland, Ruth thought. Out loud she said, "Hi, Hugh. Hello, Bing."

Bing dazzled her with a perfect smile. "Hello, Mrs. Budge. How are the Fog Festival preparations getting on?"

"Fairly well, I'd say. Hugh, your father needs help unloading the truck."

Hugh nodded, consulting a watch bristling with knobs and dials. "Okay. I'll see you around, Bing. Is Dimple here yet, Ruth? I've got something for her."

"I think she said she'd be here around ten."

He nodded again. "See you later."

"I understand you're in the bait business," Bing said. "I'd love to get some fishing in while I'm here."

"Come on by. I can supply all the bait you could ever need. I live in a cottage down below. Just follow the squawking bird sounds."

Ruth said good-bye and continued working her way through the room. Several contest officials were roaming around making notes on clipboards. It seemed that Maude didn't have to twist any arms to round up judges. Officer Katz looked thrilled to be wearing a Fog Cook-off Judge T-shirt as he poked his nose into various bubbling pots. Ruth snapped a shot of him frowning at the clipboard.

"Hello, Nate. How did you get roped into judging?"

"Oh, I volunteered when Mrs. Stone said you needed another judge. What could be a better job than judging a food contest?" He inhaled. "Do you smell that? I can't figure out what it is, but it smells awesome."

Her nostrils were working overtime trying not to let the amazing scents distract her mental processes. "I don't know, but I'm going to find out. See you later."

Her heart quickened when she caught sight of her husband behind his cooking station.

"Hello, honey," Monk bellowed. He left his spot behind the portable stove and planted a big kiss on her lips. "I've missed you today."

She melted into his embrace. "I've missed you, too." Looking over his shoulder, she added, "I didn't know you had decided on a recipe."

"You betcha. Are you here to get a shot of the winning dish?" He grinned. "Then come on over and take a look."

"A little confident, aren't we? What are you cooking?"

"It's truffled new potatoes. Very simple recipe, but guaranteed to knock you into another dimension." His close-cropped gray hair was stippled with sweat, and his face shone with enthusiasm.

It pleased her to watch him cook. She found it amazing that such huge, calloused hands could hold the kitchen instruments so delicately, like a jeweler setting precious stones. But he was a man full of surprising contradictions.

"Do you mind if I taste?"

"Nah, go right ahead. Those are the very best French black truffles. They oughta be, for what I paid for them."

Ruth looked at the pot and then back at her

husband. "Black truffles?"

She flashed back to the boxful that Hugh had shown her at the park, and their conversation about the price they brought. They were so strange and exotic. Ed Honeysill would have enjoyed this, she thought with a pang. "Where did you get them?"

"From Hugh. He got them for me at a discount, if you can call one hundred fifty dollars a discount. I don't usually cook with truffles, so the price kind of hit me by surprise. I figured it would be a shoo-in recipe for the contest."

Ruth shook her head and sipped the spoonful. It was indeed scrumptious. "Are you looking to win that trip to Half Moon Bay?" she asked.

"Sure. But only if my lovely bride goes with me."

She smiled and busied herself with her camera, wondering when the thrill of being adored by this wonderful man would wear off. God loved her without a doubt to have blessed her with two amazing husbands in one lifetime.

"Did Hugh tell you who his source is?"

"No. Trade secret, I think."

Ruth caught sight of Dimple lugging a crate of luminous mushrooms to the supply table in the back of the room.

"Gotta go, Monk. I'll talk to you later."

Dimple heaved her box onto the table and stood there. Her fingers absently stroked the smooth mushroom caps.

Ruth hesitated. "Are you okay?"

She looked up, unfocused for a moment. "Oh,

Ruth. Hello. I am okay, just thinking. It's so strange, having her back."

"Your mother?" she asked gently.

"Yes. For so many years I imagined where she was, what she looked like." Dimple thought for a moment. "I thought she would be taller."

Ruth smiled. "Did she say anything—about why she came back, I mean?"

"She said she wrote me several notes over the years, saying she regretted leaving me, and that she tried to keep in touch with calls, but Daddy threw away the cards and wouldn't allow me to talk to her."

Ruth could easily see that happening with a hardened man like Buster.

"Then she found out that I had a baby. She said she booked a flight twice to come and see me but each time she canceled." Dimple took a soft bristled brush from her pocket and gently whisked it over the mushroom caps. "Fear drains the vigor of intention."

"Uh, yes. I am sure that's true."

"She had the car accident, and it changed her priorities, she said."

"Does your mother—" Ruth stopped. "Is she going to stay in Finny?"

"I don't think so. She has a beautiful house in Arizona and a husband who dotes on her, she says. Not like Daddy at all. I just think she wants to get to know me, us."

Ruth felt guilty for the relief that flooded through her. The woman was going home! Ruth refocused her thoughts. "How are you feeling about it all? About your mother coming back?"

Dimple gathered her long hair into a bundle, loosely braiding it, and draped it over one shoulder. "I am not sure. It is so strange to have a mother again, after being an orphan for so long."

Ruth knew that Buster had all but washed his hands of his daughter when she became pregnant, leaving her, for all intents and purposes, parentless. "I'm no expert or anything, but I'm sure it's just fine to feel confused and unsure. It may take some time for you two to get acquainted again." She was pleased with her advice. Sometimes spending an afternoon watching Oprah paid off.

Ruth noticed a slim metallic cylinder on the table. "What's this?"

"It's a digital recorder for recording my observations as I check the polytunnel. Hugh gave it to me. Wasn't that nice?"

Ruth nodded. "It looks expensive." Maybe Hugh had finally come up with a moneymaking idea after all.

"Ruth," Dimple began, gazing absently out the window.

"Yes?"

"Why do you suppose a barbecued chicken just came flying out the opening of that tent?"

Ruth stared out the window into the lot next door. She was unable to fathom a reasonable explanation as a plate of jelly doughnuts followed the chicken.

9

Jack's car squealed to a stop, followed closely by Nate's and Mary's vehicles. They could see the sides of the tent undulating and the sound of screaming.

Alva came trotting out of the tent opening, a red stickiness dripping from his hair down the front of his plaid shirt.

"You're bleeding!" Jack said. He grabbed the old man and pushed him away from the tent.

"Nah, just hot sauce. I got off ten shots with the squeeze bottle before I took any." His face was wreathed in a huge grin. "It's a frenzy in there. Ain't seen anything like it since Korea."

Jack handed him to Mary, who steered Alva out of harm's way. The two uniformed officers then stood ready at one side of the tent opening, and Jack, in jeans with a badge clipped to his belt, moved to the other side. They did a slow count to three and plunged into the craziness.

Bodies were flying everywhere. Some launched food at each other; others hid behind overturned tables. Hugh stood on top of the long rectangular serving table shouting something at the top of his lungs, whopping anybody he could reach with a soup ladle. Jack could just make out Bing crouched under the table next to him.

"What in the world—?" Mary shouted as a square of lasagna hurtled through the air and hit the side of her head. "Who did that?" She grabbed the nearest human form, which turned out to be a dark-haired youth, one of the Coastal Comets acrobatic troupe. Hauling him to a nearby table, she cuffed him to the metal legs.

Nathan was attempting to intervene between the Sassie sisters and the giant of a man they were bouncing up and down upon.

"Get off me, you sacks of lard. I ain't even from this jerkwater town," the man wheezed.

"Sacks of lard?" one of the gray-haired women said in between bounces. "Just who do you think you are?"

"Ladies, let's just take it easy here," Nate began. "I'm sure the guy can apologize if you let him get some oxygen in his lungs."

Jack saw Evelyn crawl under tables along the perimeter of the tent, trying to feel her way to the exit. "Oh yuck," she muttered. "I can't believe this is happening."

Jack jumped over puddles of chili and smears of barbecued chicken carnage as he made his way over toward the only fully upright people in the tent. He slipped on a ketchup-dampened patch of grass and slid on his belly, coming to a stop at the feet of Maude Stone and Bubby Dean.

"My fault?" Maude shouted over the din. "How is this my fault?"

"Because," Bubby shouted back, "this was your crazy idea to put up a tent for these lunatics. Some of them aren't Finny people, Maude. You can't predict what these nutcases will do in our town." A glob of custard quivered on the edge of his left eyebrow.

"Alva saw a bunch of them wackos headed up nose last night. Wearing bandannas and all. He says they think people are ruining the earth, and they're looking for a sacrificial victim to make an example of. I'm beginning to think he's right," Bubby bellowed. Then he added, "Maybe we should offer you up."

She ignored the last comment. "That's a load of hogwash. Alva is a crazy old geezer, and you are, too, for believing him." Maude ducked to avoid an airborne biscuit. "And what about you? It was your idea to host a luncheon in a tent, for Pete's sake. What about that cockamamy idea?"

"That's enough, you two," Jack said, clambering up from his prone position. Neither one looked down.

"That was a great idea. The council approved it. Don't try to shift this fiasco to my door." Bubby ducked too slowly to avoid the chicken thigh that followed the biscuit. It splatted on the back of his neck and slid forlornly down his T-shirt.

Maude finally noticed Jack. "Jack? It's about time. Just what in the world are you going to do about this mess?" Maude said. She flicked some spaghetti off her shoulder. "Is this the sort of behavior we tolerate in this town?"

"That's pretty highfalutin of you to say," Bubby yelled to the top of her head. "Finny was doing just fine before this idiot festival."

Jack slid back down to a kneeling position as he temporarily lost his footing again. "Just simmer down."

"Fine? You call finding a toe fine?" Her voice

rose to a spine-tingling screech. "It's only a matter of time before they find the body that goes with it, you knucklehead. Then we'll have two murders on our hands."

"Knucklehead?" His face turned crimson. "You are the most—"

Jack made it to his feet. "Enough already!" he exploded. "Take it outside and sit down until I get there!"

Bubby and Maude started, looking at the detective. Without a word they both made their way out of the tent.

Jack put his fingers into his mouth and blew. Hard. The blast pierced through the din. The entire congregation froze in various awkward positions as if they were engaged in a violent Twister game.

"Listen up. I'm Detective Jack Denny from the Finny Police Department. You will all remove your hands from each other and walk out of this tent. When you exit this area, sit yourselves down outside on the field and wait until an officer tells you to go. Now move it!"

The sticky horde ambled out of the tent until only the officers and the young acrobat handcuffed to the table remained.

Jack's T-shirt and jeans were soaked and grass stained. Mary Dirisi was trying in vain to push the stringy cheese out of her face. Nathan was covered from forehead to boots with a combination of cherry cola and potato salad.

"And they say nothing ever happens in Finny,"

Nathan said. A drop of soda collected in his mustache before it fell onto his shirtfront.

"Yeah, well," Jack said, "I'll take murder and mayhem over a food fight any day." As the words came out of his mouth, he felt a quiver of unease deep in his gut.

He slogged after the greasy crowd streaming out of the tent. Mary and Nate plopped the messy people into groups and wrote down pertinent information in their slightly sticky notebooks.

Jack noticed Evelyn and Rocky standing away from the group, talking quietly with their heads together. He edged closer when he noticed Ruth sidle up to them. He stopped to help a teen with noodles in his hair pick up several plates off of the ground. All the while Jack kept his ears tuned in to Ruth's conversation.

"Are you all right?" Ruth asked.

Evelyn looked up, her face smeared with a tomato-based product. "I can't believe it. I didn't mean to start a brawl. I just got so mad, I threw a dinner roll at him and it smacked some other guy instead. Before I knew it, there was food flying everywhere."

"Who were you angry with?"

Rocky answered first. "That jerk, Mitchell," Rocky barked. "He deserves a lot more than a dinner roll in the face." He swiped at a strand of spaghetti hanging from his narrow chin. "Where is he? He needs to be taught a lesson."

"Never mind, Rocky. It's over for now." Evelyn took a steadying breath. "I told you about the man who mutilated Peanut. Bing is the one. I was going to file a complaint with animal services, but he threatened to report me for having too many animals on my property."

"And he did anyway, Evelyn. You know it was him." He glared through the smear of mustard on the lenses of his glasses.

"I'm pretty sure, but there's no way to prove it," she said, wiping her eyes.

"If it wasn't for that low-down slimeball, I'd still have my car, too."

Jack finished stuffing the paper plates into the kid's plastic bag and came closer. "Well, it looks like we're all going to need some dry cleaning services. I couldn't help overhearing. How did Bing get your car, Rocky?"

Evelyn and Rocky looked at each other.

"Oh, it's a long story. Bing, uh, had something of ours that we wanted back, and we had to sell the car." She cleared her throat. "Anyway, it's water under the bridge now." The silver strands in her dark hair shimmered in the waning sunlight. "He's just so arrogant, so cruel. He asked me about my 'crippled mongrel' as if he had nothing to do with it. I just couldn't stand it."

"It's all right, Ev." Rocky put his arm around her shoulder. "Nothing awful happened, just a food fight." Rocky took several deep breaths. "Let's center ourselves."

Jack looked at the mottled flush on Rocky's face and figured he would require much more than deep breathing to center anything. They moved away and sat down on a log to wait for their turn with the police.

"Not bad," Jack said.

Ruth looked at the sticky detective. "What's not bad?"

He brushed a lettuce leaf out of his hair. "You are a pretty good snoop, I must admit. I don't think they'll be inclined to share that much information with law enforcement."

"Maybe not when you're dressed like a salad."

"Funny. I think they'd clam up even without the garnish."

"It's the motherly aura I exude," she said with a grin. "For some reason, people share their secrets with me."

"Let me know if you need some contract work with the Finny police." He smiled and walked back into the throng, wondering what Bing could have taken from the Bippos that would require them to sell a car to buy it back. He took another glance at the chaos. The misty air seemed to envelop the group, leaving Rocky and Evelyn framed against the foggy backdrop. Rocky reached to hug her and his shirt rode up in the back. Jack made a note to find out why Mr. Rocky Bippo had a knife tucked in his waistband.

As he turned away, his heart skidded to a stop. Bobby stood there, looking very clean in a white T-shirt and sweat pants. She flashed him a wide smile.

"Hello, Detective. I was just going for a run, but I couldn't resist poking my nose in all this mayhem." Her eyes traveled across his splattered shirt. "Looks like you've been right in the thick of it."

He felt a sudden shortness of breath. "It's been an interesting morning." He looked at her bob of silky hair and remembered the goo that was no doubt coating him from head to toe at the moment. *Conversation.*

Make some conversation, he told himself.

"So, uh, running, eh?" He shoved his hands into his pockets, ignoring the avalanche of noodles that fell to the grass as he did so. "Running is good, yeah." *That was smooth, Denny.*

She laughed. The sound was high and musical. "It's good, yeah. Do you run?"

"Me?" He tried to remember the last time he went jogging. It might have been the fitness test at the police academy. "Running. Yes, I do running. I mean, I jog. Yes." It was only when he needed to chase down a suspect, but that was running, wasn't it? He tried hard to think of a way to extend the conversation.

"Maybe we could go running this week. On your day off or something," she said.

His heart began to jackhammer again. "Yes," he said too loudly. "Yes, let's run this week."

She nodded. Then she leaned forward and raised a hand to his hair. He held his breath as her fingers brushed his cheek. She smelled like vanilla.

"Okay. But maybe you should leave the pickles at home." She handed him the slice of dill and jogged off, her laughter trailing behind her.

10

The morning shower was as hot as Ruth could stand it. As she watched the suds swirl around her toes, she could not get the memory of the crumpled balloon out of her mind. It was Wednesday, a scant five days after the balloon accident, and she could still hear the awful thump as the basket hit the ground. She had seen Ed so very much alive a few hours before the launch that she could not reconcile the picture of the congenial bald man with the twisted mass of flesh imbedded in Finny's Nose.

The food fight the day before did nothing to ease the atmosphere. She didn't know whether to laugh or cry at the thought of all those grown-ups hurling food at each other like a bunch of preschoolers.

Idly she wondered what the cultured Meg Sooner had made of the whole sticky mess.

Ruth stayed in the shower until the water became tepid, but she still could not focus her mind on anything but the current string of worries. She wished Monk was home, but the catering business demanded plenty of hours. Determined to snap out of her funk, she prepared a cup of near-scalding coffee and sat down at the table with the decrepit journal.

August the 25th, 1923
    It's all coming back to me now. It was two months ago when the old lady showed up. No

one remembered letting her in, but there she was, a wizened old China lady. Her front teeth were gone and most of her hair. She was dressed from head to toe in a dreadful black shift with a huge crocheted shawl that seemed to swallow her up. She pointed a bony finger at me and croaked, "Where is she? Where is my Ling?"

I told her Ling was gone. Slats sent her away a month ago because she wasn't able to keep up with the dance steps. Ling wasn't much of a looker to start with, and she just kept getting thinner and thinner until there wasn't anything left to do the kicks and turns. Her dance costumes hung on her like rags. I felt bad for Ling, but she took it well. Just packed her bags and left.

"You get her back!" the old lady shrieked, still jabbing her finger in the air.

By then all the girls were crowded around on account of the screaming.

I told the old gal that Ling was gone, and I didn't know where, but she continued to scream in a most unholy way. Finally, my piano man grabbed hold of her arms and drug her out. The screams echoed throughout the restaurant.

I don't know why it's come into my mind again. Maybe it's this evil fog that has been smothering us in darkness for weeks. I can't get her screams out of my mind.

Ruth read the passage twice, struggling against the

loops and curves of the penned script. It was a fantastic tale so far. A Finny woman, working for a gangster, watching the developing loves and lives of her dancing girls. It had all the makings of a tragic soap opera.

Reading the journal was an attempt to distract herself, but it had only stirred her mind even further. Could the woman's story be true? Ruth knew that in the early twenties there was indeed an eating establishment on the outskirts of Finny. And it was certainly true that Finny was named after an unsuccessful rumrunner. Ruth needed to find out if the journal was fact or fancy. She remembered her earlier idea to visit Ellen Foots.

Picking up the phone, she dialed the Finny Public Library and made arrangements to sit in on Ellen's next presentation later in the afternoon.

After hanging up, she waded through her birds in the backyard. "All right, everyone. Here's breakfast." She heaved a tray full of bread scraps and vegetable chunks onto the patio and left the birds to their squabbling. While they were distracted, she turned her attention to her business demands.

The worms in the fattening bed were in wiggly ecstasy as she fed them their mash. She tried to keep her mind fully engrossed in the task at hand as she moved from feeding to harvesting. The standing orders for worm castings needed to be filled regardless of the latest Finny catastrophe.

The regular beds were moist but not sticky. Just right, she thought with pride. With a flathead shovel she carefully removed the first five inches of soil where most of the worms congregated. She placed the shovelfuls on a plywood sheet covered with plastic and switched on the halogen light that dangled just above the wood. As the worms sought to escape the brightness, they began burrowing down nearer the bottom.

Ruth whisked away the top two inches of soil with a small broom and dustpan, emptying the contents into gallon drums. She waited patiently for worms to burrow down deeper and repeated her whisking. Eventually she had the required amount of worm compost for the latest orders and a solid mass of grumpy worms on her plywood.

"Go away, Teddy," she said, shoving a plump gray gull away with her shoe. She slid the worms back into the concrete bins and covered them with bird manure, topsoil, and garden compost. The cleaning up was not quite finished when the phone rang. The voice on the other end came through the receiver with piercing decibels.

"You've got to get to the tent. The Bippo woman is doing a presentation for the natives, and you have to get a few pictures."

"Maude, are you sure? The last event turned into a culinary brawl. Maybe we should cancel the rest of the festival activities."

"Ruth Marilyn Budge. If you think for one minute we are canceling the rest of the festival, you've gone around the bend. We've spent big bucks on that tent, and the booths, not to mention the cotton candy and popcorn machines, and that jumpy house thing—which now needs to be repaired."

Ruth held the phone away from her ear to lessen the screech. "I see your point. I was just thinking about propriety."

"Who cares about propriety? Ed Honeysill is past caring, and we've got craftspeople from up and down the coast who paid for two full weekends of festival. We will carry on as planned until we wrap up Sunday at 5:00 p.m. Besides, the next batch of visitors won't even know there's been a murder unless we make a big deal about it."

Ruth found that hard to believe. "Okay, Maude. I can stop by the tent on the way to snap a few pictures." She hung up hurriedly before Maude had time to ask her to wear the Mrs. Fog costume.

Evelyn stood at the podium in front of the sparse crowd. It was a quiet, dazed-looking group that gathered in the tent, mostly silent except for the occasional furtive whisper regarding the previous day's culinary brawl. Behind Evelyn hung a banner announcing THE DOG HOUSE in red felt letters. As she spoke, she stroked a raggedy bundle under her arm. Occasionally the bundle poked a wet nose into the air and sniffed.

Ruth waved to Mary Dirisi. With all that had been happening lately, the more police around the better, even if they were out of uniform and on their day off. She turned on the camera.

She didn't even have time to raise it to her eye before Bing strode into the tent, taking a position near the entrance. Just as quickly, Ruth saw Rocky in jeans and a sweatshirt march down the aisle to him.

"You've got some nerve showing up here like you're some sort of dog lover," Rocky snarled in a not-so-soft whisper. His face was mottled, and his eyes flashed through the thick lenses of his glasses.

"I can show up anywhere I want," Bing barked. "And I am a lover of dogs. Normal dogs, not mental cases."

Ruth tensed and glanced at Mary. Evelyn continued to speak, her eyes fastened on the two men at the back of the tent. The dogs peered curiously from behind the short fences fastened together in makeshift kennels.

"Rudy, for instance, would be an excellent dog for a house with older children." Her words seemed as though they came out on autopilot. "He's an energetic fellow, but with training he would become a loyal family friend."

Heads began to turn toward the ruckus in the back. Mary frowned. "Did you say the dogs are fixed before they are adopted out?" she asked loudly, perhaps to assert her presence, Ruth thought.

"Yes, that's a requirement to ensure we don't increase the number of unwanted animals in the world."

"What are you, some kind of stalker?" Rocky snapped.

"The only person stalking anyone is you, you freak," Bing said with a laugh.

"Do you do any consulting on dog training?" Bubby asked between nervous slugs of coffee. "My dachshund, Inky, has the worst habit of trying to eat the mailman. I have to pick up my mail at the post office now. It's a real pain in the caboose."

Evelyn was just opening her mouth to reply when Rocky threw a punch that caught Bing under the chin and sent him over backward. With blood oozing from his mouth, Bing recovered and dove for him.

They both went over in a heap.

Evelyn raced down the center aisle. The three penned dogs in front of the podium leaped over their enclosure and followed, their barks deafening the audience.

"Man," Mary said. She got calmly to her feet and joined the fracas.

"Stop! Rocky! Stop!" Evelyn screamed, trying to grab hold of Rocky's arm. Her brother continued to slam his fist into Bing's ribs.

"Get off me, you psychopath!" Bing shouted with a kick that sent Rocky's glasses spiraling through the air. "Don't you have any more buildings to blow up?"

Ruth put her camera on a folding chair and joined Bubby and a few others trying to corral the yapping dogs.

Mary grabbed hold of Rocky's ponytail where it connected to the scalp and yanked him upward. He came with a grunted obscenity and fists raised to strike his new assailant. Catching sight of the look on her face, he reconsidered.

"Sit there," she commanded, pointing to a chair. To Bing she said, "You, get up. Step outside." Bing also followed directions and walked out of the tent. "I'll be back to talk to you in a minute," she said to Rocky. "If you move, I'm going to have to come after you, and I'm already irritated."

He watched her go while Evelyn held a handkerchief against a cut on his eyebrow.

Ruth finally managed to grab hold of the smallest of the canine escapees. She took a leisurely pace back toward the pen, giving her plenty of time to eavesdrop on the conversation developing just outside the tent opening.

"What's the problem between you two?" Mary demanded.

"There's no—" Bing began.

"Can the nonsense. It's my day off, and this is the last thing I want to be doing, so get to it."

"All right. We had a disagreement last year. Rocky blames me for abusing a dog I adopted from Evelyn."

Bing saw Mary's eyebrows rise in disgust and added, "I didn't do anything to the dog. I gave him back because he was nuts."

"And?"

"And Rocky blames me for reporting Evelyn to the authorities for having too many dogs on her property."

"And?"

"And I didn't do it. Rocky's as nuts as the dog. The guy is a few eggs short of a dozen, you know what I mean?" Bing smiled warmly. "You should run a check on him. He's been linked to some of that ecoterrorism stuff, you know."

Ruth thought about her late-night Internet research

as she lingered near the tent opening.

"Go home," Mary said. "I'll come and get you if I need to haul either of your butts in." She turned back into the tent.

Ruth busied herself making sure the dog's collar was securely fastened.

Rocky pushed Evelyn's hand away from his eye and stood. "Officer, Mitchell is harassing me and my sister," he said.

"Sit down. He says you're mad over the dog thing last year. What's the deal?" Mary zipped her windbreaker against a breeze that wafted into the now-empty tent.

"He beat our dog last year and mutilated him," Rocky snarled. He blinked nearsightedly up at the officer.

"Did you press charges?"

Evelyn and Rocky looked at each other. "No," she mumbled.

"Why not?"

"Because he said he'd turn Ev in to animal control for housing too many dogs." Rocky wiped the blood away from his eye with his sleeve. "Funny how animal control got an anonymous tip a month later anyway."

"Okay, so we've got your word and his word. What happened just now to make you two lose your minds and start swinging?"

"He was leering at my sister, smiling in that playboy arrogant way. He doesn't have any business here. There's no way he's coming near my sister or her dogs again."

"He has as much business here as any other member of the public. What do you have to do with ecoterrorism?"

Rocky's mouth opened and closed. After a moment he said, "Nothing. I don't know anything about that."

Mary eyed him closely. "Okay, for the moment. Now since you jokers have disrupted your sister's presentation for the day, go home and cool off. Next time you go to jail."

Rocky shoved his bent glasses into his pants pocket and stalked off.

Mary turned to Evelyn. "Has he always been a loose cannon?"

Evelyn sighed, her thin shoulders hunched. "I guess so." She looked down at her worn loafers. "It's just because he loves me. He's really protective. My parents died when we were young. Rocky has taken care of me since I was seven."

"Has he been in trouble before?"

She hesitated. "No. Not since we were teenagers. He, uh, beat up someone years ago, a boy he thought was no good for me." Evelyn cleared her throat. "He loves me, that's all." She added softly, "He's the only one who ever has."

Mary Dirisi nodded. "Yeah, well, you know what they say, Ms. Bippo. Sometimes love hurts."

Ruth thought about the hatred in Rocky's face when he looked at Bing. She knew that Bing had something of the Bippos that they desperately wanted back.

Sometimes love hurts.

Ruth wondered if it could hurt enough to kill.

It turned into a ridiculously sunny afternoon as Ruth
hurried to the Finny Public Library. She imagined
Maude hard at work with her fog machine.

Ruth found the presentation commencing in the
back room. It consisted of a fatigued-looking teacher
by the name of Mrs. Finkelstein and a group of
twenty-one exceptionally well-behaved third graders.
The model behavior was due not to the efforts of the
weary Finklestein but to the aura of aggressive energy
emanating from the six-foot-six librarian.

Ellen sat in a straight-backed chair, hiking boots
planted firmly on the ground, her hair a whirly confusion of black frizz that hovered around her face.

"Well then," she announced, "let's move on to the
Roaring Twenties in Finny. Does anyone know why
they are called the Roaring Twenties?"

No third grader had the internal fortitude to
attempt an answer.

"Hmm," Ellen sniffed. "Disappointing. It was due
to the exuberance and, I might add, moral degradation
that accompanied the constitutional amendment which
outlawed the sale or purchase of alcoholic beverages. It
was a dangerous time to live here. Plenty of lawlessness
and chaos."

Ruth noticed the children's eyes beginning to
glaze over and roll back into their youthful heads as
the librarian continued her historical diatribe. The

glaze seemed to have infected Ruth's own eyes until a particular word caused her to start upright.

"— *murder*," Ellen said.

Mrs. Finkelstein sat up straight also, as though someone had slapped her. She adjusted her wire-rimmed glasses and swept the short bangs out of her eyes to get a better look at the speaker.

"I'm sure your teacher has told you about the Pickle Jar, which used to stand just below the tip of Finny's Nose. It was run by a woman named Pickles Peckenpaugh who came to Finny from San Francisco in 1922."

A tiny voice ventured out from a boy in the front row. "Who got murdered? Was there bodies and everything?"

Ruth looked over the children's heads to see Mrs. Finklestein gesturing wildly with a slashing motion across her throat and violent head shaking.

"Well, for goodness' sake, they're old enough to know the truth. It was a pretty brutal way to die, I'll admit."

The children were warming to the subject, encouraged by the fact that their classmate had not been slain. A chubby girl with a complicated array of braids spoke up. "How did it happen?"

"Oh, it was a mysterious case. Two terrible crimes occurred on Finny's Nose in 1923."

Crimes? Ruth leaned forward.

"The first was a young girl, tied to a tree and nearly burned to death in September of 1923, if I recall correctly. She was a dancing girl at the Pickle Jar.

Rescued just in time. Terrible thing having someone try to set you on fire. Seems like shooting or strangling would be more humane."

Ruth noted Mrs. Finkelstein squinching her eyes together as she slipped down in her chair. There was a buzz of excitement from the kids.

"Then exactly one week later, there was a body found in the very same spot. A man, with his neck broken. He was believed to be the ringleader of a gang. The killer was never caught. What have I told you about gangs, children? A sure way to get your throat slit."

For the next fifteen minutes, they looked at grainy slides that Ellen projected onto the wall.

Ellen slapped her hands on her thighs. "Well then, that concludes my presentation, and it's time to check out a book before you leave. Except for you, Hugo." She pointed an accusing finger at a gangly boy in the back row. "You will not check out another thing from this library until you return *The Ultimate Adventures of Spider-Man*."

Since the teacher appeared to be out of commission, no doubt mentally reworking her résumé, the librarian rallied the troops and had them line up at the door to leave. Ruth joined her caboose to the end of the line. "What happened to the Pickle Jar?" she asked over the gabble of voices.

"It closed down after the murder and fell into disrepair. All that's left is a pile of foundation stones halfway up nose." She turned her attention to the hapless Hugo as the class began to file out of the meeting room. "You, young man, will have to dust the shelves while the others are checking out books. And there's a bulletin board that needs the staples removed." Then the ferocious librarian was gone, leaving a wiggly bunch of lined-up third graders and a dazed-looking woman feebly trying to rise from her chair.

───

Over a cup of coffee with extra cream and sugar, Ruth opened the diary again.

August the 27ᵗʰ, 1923
Received a letter from Slats today. He is on his way to Finny and I am to expect him tomorrow. He says he knows who pinched his money and he's coming to settle the score. My blood runs cold and I haven't been able to swallow a morsel. I must get word to Soapy Dan somehow. He must take to his heels before Slats arrives. I simply must reach him before Slats does.

August the 28th, 1923
Slats arrived this morning with two of his thugs. He asked Janey most politely if she knew of Dan's whereabouts. Janey told him things had ended between them before Dan skipped town. Slats spoke to all of us calmly as though he hadn't a care in the world. Maybe things will be all right if Soapy Dan does indeed disappear for a while. Perhaps things will be all right after all.

September the 7th, 1923

*I cannot even force my horror into words.
What I saw last night is burned into my brain
and will stay there forever. I came down to open
the doors in the morning, and Hazel met me in
the kitchen.*

"She's gone, Pickles!"

*I threw on some clothes and woke Roscoe.
By then most of the other girls were there and
we headed up Finny's Nose, following the awful
shrieking. We were almost to the top when we
saw her there, tied to a pine. She looked so small
and white in the midst of that poisonous fog.
I almost didn't see her at first until the needles
under her feet caught.*

*As I live and breathe, I will never forget the
sound of that whooshing flame, or the look in
her eyes as she watched her skirt begin to burn.*

*Roscoe and I ran forward to try to undo the
ropes. We managed to drag her away just before
the fire exploded everywhere. Her face was
untouched, but her arms and legs were burned.
I could see terror and anguish in her eyes. We
could all feel the terrible evil settling into the
air around us. Only God can mend the horror
in our hearts.*

*This place will forever echo with the
screams of that poor girl.*

The ruins of the Pickle Jar could have been passed
over completely unnoticed by the casual observer. As
it was, Ruth almost missed them. The charred beams

were nearly covered by a scalp of brilliant green grass, a tint of green found only in rare tropical frogs and play dough. Here and there a pile of crumbling bricks dotted the small plateau, and a fallen tree surrendered to the onslaught of decay.

Ruth and Cootchie trudged almost to the top of Finny's Nose for their pre-dinner outing in order to get a more aerial view of what used to be Finny's most infamous eating establishment. Ruth planted her bottom on a spongy trunk and hoisted Cootchie up next to her.

"Juice?" the little girl inquired.

"Okay, sweet pea." Ruth fished around in her backpack and found a sippy cup full of pomegranate juice. She handed it to the child along with a handful of soybeans. Cootchie slurped away, picking long stalks of grass with her free hand.

Looking downslope, she saw that the plateau ambled along for several hundred yards before it dropped away gradually into a wooded depression with a creek running through it. In the spring, the creek swelled to a respectable width until summer came and reduced it to a series of shallow puddles. Now it barely burbled along. Cootchie hopped off her perch and put down her juice cup before beginning to further excavate a gopher hole nearby.

Ruth's thoughts turned to a diary entry she had read earlier. She had not yet finished reading it, but the horrendous description of Janey's attack stayed in her mind, along with Ellen's retelling of the murder. A cluster of pines above her head made her wonder if this might have been the spot where the unfortunate girl had been tied.

"Enough of this. Let's go home, Cootchie."

There was no answer.

Ruth jumped up. She looked behind the log and scanned the slope in all directions for the child. "Cootchie, where are you?" she called.

The only sound was the wind against the leaves.

She continued to call out with increasing volume and intensity until she was screaming louder than she ever had in her life.

A paralyzing panic squeezed her heart and lungs. "Cootchie! Cootchie, where are you? Cootchie, answer Nana Ruth!" she shouted. Her frantic cries echoed among the trees.

"Dear God, please let me find her." Her legs pounded over rocks and branches as she ran down the slope to the spot where she left her backpack. Grabbing her cell phone with shaking hands, she dialed 911.

"Please help me. It's Ruth Budge. I'm at the top of Finny's Nose and Cootchie has disappeared." Her shaking fingers almost lost their grip on the phone. "Please, please help me. I can't find her anywhere."

As she stood with the phone pressed to her ear, her eyes scanned desperately for a glimpse of the girl's blue checked shirt.

The only splash of color was the tiny cup, sitting on the log, the juice gleaming blood red in the sun.

The next several hours passed in an agonizingly slow creep. There were lights and sirens, people in uniform and one in an apron. They asked her questions, came and left with radios and phones. Someone made her sit down once again on the spongy log. The aproned person with a ladle in his pocket sat next to her. It took her a minute to realize it was her husband.

"It's going to be okay," Monk said, putting a beefy arm around her shoulders. "They're going to find her."

His voice seemed to come from a long way off.

The sun was behind the trees, and a chill fog rose to meet it.

A car wheezed up the slope and came to rest in a cloud of dust several yards from the log. Dimple and her mother stepped out.

Meg held Dimple by the arm, leading her as one would an elderly person. Dimple's face was very white.

As the two women approached, Ruth rose to her feet like a marionette controlled by some unseen hand. She looked into Dimple's eyes and saw a horror that took the words out of her mouth. There was no anger there, but a look of such profound fear that it made Ruth's throat go dry.

They stood there for a tortured moment of silence.

Meg clutched Dimple's arm more tightly. "We understand you took Cootchie up here."

Ruth nodded. Tears welled up and spilled down her face.

"Cootchie must have wandered away while Ruth's back was turned," Monk said.

Meg regarded him for a moment, her gray eyes

narrowed. "Her back shouldn't have been turned."

Somewhere down deep Ruth registered surprise at the anger she heard in Meg's voice.

"Now wait just a minute, ma'am. Ruth has taken excellent care of Cootchie since the day she was born," he said.

"She didn't take very good care of her today, did she?" Her voice was shrill and hovered oddly in the rising fog.

"That's not fair, ma'am. You haven't been here to see how well Ruth cares for Cootchie."

Before Meg had a chance to respond, Jack approached and cleared his throat. "Ladies, I have something to tell you. It may be nothing at all, but I think you should know a witness saw a pickup driving down the fire trail on the far side of Finny's Nose."

They all stared at the detective.

Monk spoke first. "Who was the witness? Did he see a child in the truck?"

"It was one of the Coastal Comets, a guy named Hector Rodriguez. He was hiking and says he saw a pickup headed downslope about an hour ago. He has no details about the driver." Jack looked down at the faded knees of his jeans. "We found these on the ground near the fire trail." Slowly he held up a plastic bag. Inside were three soybeans.

Dimple buried her face in her mother's shoulder, and Ruth slid to the hard ground of Finny's Nose.

12

Jack collapsed in his squeaky chair at his desk, convinced that if the coffee machine wasn't repaired soon, he would have to shoot someone. The desperation he felt at not being able to find Cootchie only deepened when the pair from the FBI showed up to take over the search. It was now well into Thursday and still no progress. He thought constantly about his own young son. It was all he could do not to pick up the phone and call Louella to check on him again.

His stomach growled, reminding him he had not eaten lunch.

The phone rang, and he snatched it up. His face warmed when he heard the voice on the other end. "Oh, hey, Bobby."

"Hi, Jack. Is there any news?"

"No." He hoped his helplessness didn't seep into his voice. "It's pretty much the FBI's show now."

"I bet that really ticks you off."

He smiled. How did she know that? "Yeah, I guess it does. Are Monk and Ruth okay?"

"I don't think so. They won't be okay until there is word, I think."

"Me neither."

"Well," Bobby said, "I just wanted to tell you that I hope you're holding up. I know this is hard for you. Maybe we can go for that run after everything is settled and Cootchie is back safe and sound."

His heart jumped. "Oh sure. I would love that."

"When do you get to come home?"

He groaned. "Who knows."

"Okay. I'll fix you a frittata and leave it at your house. Do you like fritattas?"

He had no clue what a frittata was, but that didn't stifle the warm feeling in his gut. "Sure, that sounds great."

Nathan entered the office with a coffee cup in his hand.

"I've gotta get back to work. Thank you for checking in. I'm sure the frittata will be great." He hung up and looked at his friend. "If that's coffee, you are promoted to admiral."

"It's orange juice, and we don't have an admiral."

"Okay." He noted lines of exhaustion on Nate's face that he was sure matched his own. He struggled to pull his mind to the Honeysill investigation. "Did you catch anything from the Candace interview that I missed?"

"Nothing in particular. She came across pretty sincerely ignorant about the life insurance policy."

"It gives her a motive for killing him," Jack said.

"Two hundred fifty thousand motives, I'd say. Do you want the background on Rocky Bippo that Mary dug up?"

"Sure," he said wearily. "Let me have it."

Nate consulted a sheaf of papers. "He's a GOP."

"A Republican?"

"A Guardian of the Planet. Some sort of gang that goes around trying to keep people from cutting down trees and stuff like that."

"Legal or not?"

"He's been connected with blockading a logging road and dumping sawdust and a three-hundred-pound stump in the middle of an Oregon city council office. No charges filed due to lack of evidence. Oh, here's a good one. He was in the vicinity of the Elegant Tree Farm when it was torched."

"I thought they liked trees."

"Apparently these trees were propagated from genetically modified stock."

"And that's a bad thing?" Jack asked.

"I'll bet the GOPs think so."

He rubbed his face. "That's all we need. A bunch of environmental wackos on the loose in Finny."

Jack looked at his phone again, willing it to ring with news about Cootchie. "Who's next?"

"Bing the balloon guy again. He was supposed to be the one to take Honeysill up in the balloon, but he was AWOL at launch time. We got his basic story already, but he's back for round two."

They walked to the interview room and settled into hard chairs.

The door opened, and Bing stepped into the room. He looked like a man entering a country club rather than a squad room. His hair was spiked with gel, and his muscled arms were tanned under his blue polo shirt. To top it off, the man was carrying a styrofoam cup of coffee.

"How are you?" he said to the officers, extending a hand to both. "Good to see you again. Pretty nuts around here. I bet you guys are wishing this whole festival deal would pack up and leave town."

"Something like that. You remember Officer Katz. Have a seat, Mr. Mitchell."

"Great." He slid into a chair. "I've been on my feet all day. You can call me Bing. Sounds like you people are busy these days. I understand there's a kid missing."

"We're managing. Why don't you tell us again about the day your balloon crashed, Mr. Mitchell."

"Well, let's see." He took a sip of coffee. "Like I told you before, I got up around five or so—I'm an early riser. I went for a jog on the beach before I checked in with my guys to make sure they had everything under control. Then off I went in search of Starbucks. Never did find any. Had to buy this at a catering place. Can you really survive in a town without a Starbucks?" He chuckled.

"Barely," Nate commented.

Jack tried to block out the enticing aroma of coffee. "Where were you at launch time? The balloon was scheduled to go up at one o'clock. It left without you."

"Hey, I was just seeing the sights in this little burg. It's great here, just like Mayberry or something. I'm thinking of buying a piece of property. I think this would be a great place to set up shop. Folks would pay well to see the coastline from a hot air balloon."

"What sights were you seeing, exactly?"

"I can't recall minute by minute. I spent some time on the beach, searching for the sun. Then I went for a walk. I lost all track of time—that's why I was late for the launch." He put the cup on Jack's desk and laced his fingers across his abdomen.

"Come on, gentlemen. What motive would I have for shooting down my own balloon? The things are eight grand a piece, just for the nylon skin. That would be a poor business move on my part, don't you think? Plus my best guy was up there with him. It was just a stroke of luck that he got out of it with only a broken ankle."

"We're just putting the pieces together, Mr. Mitchell. How well did you know Ed Honeysill?"

Bing looked up at the ceiling, frowning. "Let's see. I met him about two years ago at a festival in Oregon. I've seen him a couple times since; we seem to frequent the same events. I know he sold fungus or something, didn't he?"

"And how well did you know his wife?" Jack pressed.

Bing looked startled, the easy smile still in place. "Why? What did she tell you?"

"That she knows you."

"We've become friends recently. Nothing too interesting. I'm just someone she talks to when Ed is—was—networking."

"Were you with her before the launch?"

"Oh yeah. I think we talked for a while in my trailer. I don't remember what time it was or anything. I forgot about it."

"You talked?"

Bing raised an eyebrow. "Among other things. We didn't break any laws, Detective. Maybe a few commandments, but no laws." After a moment he added, "Look. I know what you're thinking, but I've got no motive to kill Honeysill. I was getting all I wanted from Candace with him alive. You know what I mean."

Jack masked his disgust by swallowing a sip of orange juice. "Okay, Mr. Mitchell. Just one more topic. We've talked about your relationship with the Bippos. Run through it once more, if you don't mind."

"Oh boy." Bing sighed. He shook his head. "I don't really have much of a relationship with them. I adopted a dog from Evelyn, trying to be a Good Samaritan, you know? It didn't work out, so I gave him back. That's about it. I don't mix with them."

"Evelyn is pretty adamant that you abused the dog," Jack said.

"Come on, guys. Do I look like the kind of guy who tortures animals?"

Jack wanted to say that Bing looked about as nice as many of the psychotics he'd met over the years. "She says when she threatened to press charges, you reported her to animal control for having too many dogs on the property."

"That's not true. I just gave back the dog; that's all."

"She seems to think you're a real hard-hearted slimeball," Nathan spoke up. "So does her brother."

Bing twitched before his smile returned. "Just between us guys, women sometimes get a little more interested in me than I do in them."

"Are you saying Evelyn Bippo wanted a relationship with you?" Jack asked.

"She would have jumped at the chance, but she

just isn't my type. Rocky is crazy, by the way. He's one of those wackos who eat wheatgrass and refuse to use plastic shopping bags. He loves trees more than people."

Jack digested the info as best he could with no coffee in his lower GI tract. "All right, Mr. Mitchell. One more thing. You own a ninety-nine Dodge Ram pickup truck?"

"Sure do. But it's back home in Oregon. I drove my Hummer here. The gas mileage is lousy, but it's worth it knowing you can roll over any moron that gets in your way."

"All right." He stood to signal the end of the interview. "Thank you for coming in. We'll be in touch. By the way, is there anyone else, besides the Bippos, that has a problem with you?"

"I'm a very likable guy, Detective—ask anyone. I really can't think of any enemies. Why do you ask?"

"It could be that Honeysill wasn't the intended target." Jack slam-dunked the coffee cup. "Maybe you were."

Jack watched Bing leave the office, a slight look of unease on the man's face.

Nate's phone rang. Jack could feel the tension before his friend spoke a word.

"Right," Nate said, eyes wide. "We're on our way."

13

The knock on the door sounded like a gunshot. Ruth leaped to her feet, hands covering her mouth, eyes staring wildly. Monk set the cup of newly steeped tea carefully on the mantel. He nodded calmly as he said, "I'll get that, honey. It's going to be fine."

Seemingly in slow motion, the door opened, and there was Jack, standing on the doormat with his hands jammed into his pockets. "Sorry to come by so late."

"Come in." Monk ushered the man inside.

"Ruth, I've got news," he said.

She stared at him like a half-wit. A terrible smothering blanket of terror pushed at her from all sides. In her mind she heard herself screaming, but no sound came out of her mouth.

"We've found her."

Monk cleared his throat and stood up straight. He gripped Ruth around the shoulders and pulled her close. "Tell us, Jack."

"She's fine, perfectly fine. Apparently whoever took Cootchie drove up the coast to Half Moon Bay and left her on the steps of the public library. She curled up in the nonfiction section under a bench and fell asleep. The custodian found her this morning. She told him she was from Finny and wanted a book about hydroponic gardening." He smiled.

"Did Cootchie say who took her?" Monk asked.

"She didn't tell us much of anything that wasn't

about poetry or rocks. She said it was a man with glasses, though she can't say if they're reading or sunglasses. As for the vehicle, she says it was a spaceship."

"Was she—? Did he—?" Ruth stammered.

"The doctor at Eden Hospital did a thorough exam, and he said she's in mint condition. No sign of, er, injury or anything." He looked closely at her. "It's all over, Ruth. Cootchie is absolutely fine, and we're going to find the person who did this." When she did not respond, Jack added, "It wasn't your fault. No one blames you."

Ruth turned away from the two men and stared out the window at the lengthening shadows.

"Okay, Jack, thanks for coming over," Monk said.

"No problem. If there is anything you need, anything at all. . ."

"We know where to find you. I've got a pot of clam chowder simmering on the stove and a loaf of bread in the oven." Monk added more quietly, "We'll get through it."

"Maybe you could take her over to Dimple's. In a few days, I mean. Let things settle awhile."

Monk nodded. "I was thinking the same thing."

Ruth walked outside. The moist air surrounded her with an outer coldness that matched her inner chill. The fog deadened the sounds. Even the birds that rustled in the corner of the yard seemed as though they were in another world. She felt moisture on her chin from the tears coursing unnoticed down her face. In the middle of the horror came a realization that she'd been given a miracle. For a moment, the agony lessened. "Thank

You, sweet Jesus," she said as she sank to the ground and gave her tears to the fog.

—⁓—

She didn't know how long she stayed on the cold ground. Vaguely she recalled the birds poking at her hair. Monk lifted her and brought her back into the house. She knew he talked to her for a while before he hoisted her in his arms, but she could not remember any of the words. Somehow she came to be deposited in a chair in front of the glowing pellet stove with a mug of steaming Earl Grey at her elbow.

Monk gave up trying to talk after a while. He sat in a rocking chair across the area rug from her and began knitting. The soft clacking of his needles and the shushing of the yarn through his fingers kept time with the rocking. That and the clock were the only sounds.

"What are you knitting?" she finally asked. A ludicrous question, but it was all her mouth could manage.

"A sweater. Cable knit, for you," he answered. He continued to watch her, his fingers working unsupervised. "You need a new one."

"The last one you gave me is still fine."

"I know," he said. "Can I get you anything?"

"No thanks." They lapsed into relative silence again.

Ruth watched the yarn loop and curl as it transformed from skein to sleeve. It was magical almost. She watched him pull a thread and unravel a row. Suddenly her heart clenched in one aching desire. If only she could undo that minute, that one second when she had turned her back on the person she loved so dearly. The moment when she let Cootchie down. Let Dimple down. The moment when she almost destroyed them all.

The sobs returned, but there were no tears left to accompany them.

Monk put down his knitting. He handed her a box of tissues and rubbed comforting circles into her back. "It's okay, Ruth. She's fine. She's just fine."

When her sobs relented, he excused himself to tend to dinner. She watched him add cream to the clam chowder and stir it slowly. The brown bread came out of the oven and perfumed the whole house with fragrance. He set glasses of iced tea on the table along with bowls of chowder and thick slabs of bread.

Ruth was too wrung out to protest as Monk took her hand and led her to the table. "Heavenly Father, thank You for this food. Thank You for bringing Cootchie back. Thank You for your boundless love that will help us through anything. Amen." He lit a bayberry candle. "Eat something. It will help."

She struggled to get the spoon to her mouth. In spite of her emotional condition, Ruth's taste buds found the chowder delectable. She managed several spoonfuls before she gave up. Monk finished his dinner and sat back, sipping the tea and watching her.

"Why don't you tell me what you're thinking?" he said.

"I was thinking," she said word by painful word,

"that Cootchie saved my life. Or maybe it was Dimple. I'm not sure."

He nodded.

"I felt like my life was over because Phillip was gone. I thought I couldn't survive another day. Not one more day." She stared at the liquid that swirled in her glass. "I wanted to walk out the door and keep walking until I fell off the edge of the earth. Dimple found me somehow. She asked me to go with her to her first ultrasound." Ruth shook her head. "I didn't know her well, and from what I did know about her, I thought she was crazy. I mean, a woman who brews her own perfume and writes fortunes for a living?"

"Dimple is one of a kind," he agreed.

"I thought she was nuts. But she asked me to go with her. And for some reason, I did. I went because I felt God was urging me to. Just for the ultrasound. Then it was just for the Lamaze classes. And then only to see her through the delivery. Then I met Cootchie, and she became the reason for me to live." Tears began to roll down her face again. "God sent her to me so I wouldn't be alone. And then He brought me to you when I was able to love again."

Monk looked at her with an exquisitely gentle expression in his gray eyes. "Cootchie was the instrument. God showed you that you were not meant to waste all the amazing gifts you've been given."

She stared at him. "There is absolutely nothing amazing about me. I have ruined the one amazing thing in my life."

"It's going to be difficult, to overcome this. But

you will, because it isn't right to waste those gifts any more now than it was then. You're too young for that. God has given you strength because He knows you will use it to His glory."

Ruth continued to stare at him.

He sighed, "Or as my father says, life is hard, but it beats the alternative."

She began to laugh.

It was midnight before they got up from the table. She talked until there were no words or tears left. He listened to it all, commenting occasionally but mostly just nodding. He helped her up from the table and walked with her to the pellet stove to warm themselves against the evening chill.

She awakened an hour later, snuggled up against his wide back. She knew the morning would bring back the horrible trauma. But for now, she relished the warmth against her cheek and the quiet snoring that enclosed her in a comforting basket of sound.

14

The police station door crashed open early Friday morning. Jack watched from his office, a phone pressed to his ear, as Alva and Hector Rodriquez, the Coastal Comet, careened in. Mary looked up from her paperwork and walked to the front counter.

"What's up?" she asked with a suspicious look at Alva's companion.

"Me and Hector was up nose, lookin' for clues. To help find Cootchie," the old man said, breathing hard. "Hector wanted to be a private eye before he went into the acrobat business."

Hector smiled, his silver front tooth winking in the overhead lights.

"Alva," Mary began.

"Don't worry; we didn't mess up any police scenes or anything."

Hector nodded.

"Alva, I guess you didn't hear. We've already—"

"We found something," he continued. "It's a clue." With that, he heaved the mass onto the counter with a terrible crash.

Jack almost dropped the phone.

Mary shot backward in surprise. Her sudden movement knocked over the nearly empty watercooler, causing her to skid to the tile floor behind the counter. He hung up and went to assist.

Alva forged ahead. "We found it about half a mile

from the top of the nose. It's a clue for sure. First that toe shows up without a foot, and now we come upon this. Don't that seem like a pattern or something?" His watery eyes grew to Oreo size. "I know it was that gang. I seem 'em with my own eyes skulking around up there."

From behind the counter, Jack heard words and water begin to flow as he headed into the front office.

"Would you just shut up for a minute, Alva?" Mary continued grunting as she tried to regain her footing, water soaking into her pants.

Jack took his eyes off the mayhem to see Hugh push through the door. "Hey, Alva. I heard they found Cootchie. Did you. . ." He caught sight of the mass on the counter. "Oh man."

"It's a clue." Alva nodded. "What do you mean they found her? Is she okay?"

"Yes, she's fine," Jack said, trying to grab Mary's slippery wrist.

"I came here to get the word firsthand," Hugh said. "It didn't seem right to go bother Dimple about it just now. Why is there water pouring all over the floor? You got a broken pipe or something?"

"It's not a broken pipe." Mary's voice came from behind the counter as Jack tried to help her up.

"Who said that?" Hugh asked.

"The gal on the floor," Alva said. "Who you figure took the little girl, Jack? Maybe they was fixin' to get some ransom." His shaggy white eyebrows flew upwards. "Maybe one of them gangsters. What do you figure?"

"I don't know, but we'll find out," Jack said.

Nathan walked out of the back office and slipped on the growing lake of drinking water. He grabbed hold of the counter to steady himself and, in doing so, knocked a file tray full of papers, a half empty coffee cup, and the business end of Mary's phone onto the floor with a crash.

As he clung to the counter, he asked, "Mary, what are you doing on the floor?"

She finally succeeded in grasping the counter and hauling herself to her knees with Jack's help. Only her head showed above the Formica. "I'm just having my nails done, Nate. What does it look like?"

"Okeydokey," he said. "Hey, Alva. Did you hear we found Cootchie up the coast? She's not hurt or anything."

The old man's face wreathed in a wrinkly grin. "Well, that's just fine, ain't it?"

"Do they know who took her yet?" Hugh asked.

"Not yet, but we'll get him."

Hugh nodded. "Did Cootchie give you any details about the kidnapper?"

"We're still sorting through all that," Nate said.

Jack's heart sank as Maude slammed the door open and squelched into the room. She whisked her knit cap off her head. "What is all this water on the floor?"

"They got a broken pipe or something," Alva piped up.

"It's not a broken pipe!" Mary yelled over the top of the counter.

"Well," Maude said in a tone of profound disgust,

"if this isn't the most unprofessional police force I've ever seen. I just came to verify that Cootchie Dent is safe and sound—if it isn't too much to ask. Is that information accurate?"

All four people in the damp waiting room shouted in unison. *"Yes!"*

"Fine then. I'll just be on my way." She whirled on her heel and marched to the door, talking over her shoulder. "Would anyone like to explain why there is a bear trap dripping gore all over the reception desk?"

No one had an answer.

Jack was halfway done with yet another check up nose when his cell phone rang.

"Hey, Jack."

"Nate, is that mess all taken care of?" He didn't want any more visitors walking into the police station to find water on the floor and bloody animal traps on the counter.

"Clean as a whistle. Say, if you're not in the middle of something, I think you'd better meet me. I'm at Vern's place."

"What's going on?"

"Uh, well, you'd better come see for yourself. Now, would be good."

"I'm on my way. Do you need backup?"

"Nah. Just you should do it."

"Okay." He shoved the paperwork into his car and climbed in. "Be there in five."

"Make it four."

Jack sped along the winding frontage road as it bumped and twisted its way to Vern Rosario's ranch. He couldn't imagine a situation that Nate couldn't handle with his unique combination of brawn and humor.

When Jack reached the gravel driveway, he saw the amber lights of Nate's cruiser. The big man stood, thumbs tucked into his belt, talking to someone perched on a rock underneath a spreading walnut tree. The figure looked familiar.

"What's going on, Nate?" Jack caught sight of two interesting details simultaneously. The figure poised on the rock was Bobby Walker, and a denim-clad leg ending in a heavy leather work boot was hanging out of the tree.

Officer Katz stepped away from the tree and spoke to Jack, keeping his peripheral vision on Bobby and the dangling leg. "It appears to me," he said, the corners of his mustache fighting against a smile, "that this little woman treed Vern Rosario."

He stared at him. "What are you talking about?"

Still smiling, Nate continued. "Ms. Walker was out for a long hike and happened upon a Mr. Rosario putting an animal of the feline persuasion into a sack, along with a rock. As he was getting ready to carry the sack in question to the pond, Ms. Walker came onto the property to discourage Mr. Rosario from engaging in said activity."

"Uh-oh." He remembered her performance at the restaurant. "How bad?"

"The cat is fine. Vern doesn't seem any worse for wear to me, but all I've seen of him is the bottom of his boots. The vocal cords seem to be in good working order."

"Is that you, Jack?" a voice called from the tree. "It's about time. This crazy woman comes onto my property and attacks me, and you take your sweet time getting over here. Did you have to stop for a doughnut or something? Did we interrupt your nap time?"

Jack approached the tree. "Mr. Rosario, why don't you come down here, and we can sort this thing out."

"I'm not coming down until you take that nut to jail. She's guilty of trespassing and assault."

Jack left the man shouting with gusto and sat down next to Bobby.

She sat with her hands clasped under her chin, regarding him with sober brown eyes. He wished his stomach wouldn't start spiraling every time she tilted her head to one side like that.

"Hi," he said.

"Hi."

"Why don't you tell me what happened?"

She sat for a moment in silence. "I guess he's about got everything. I did trespass and assault him."

"Why exactly, Bobby?"

"He was going to drown the cat. This cat." She gestured to a cat that sat curled around her ankles. "He can't do that. Drown a cat." She spoke very calmly.

He nodded for her to continue.

"I tried to reason with him. I told him I would take the cat. He wouldn't listen; he just kept screaming and telling me to get off his property."

That did not surprise him. Vern was capable of many things, but reasoning was not way up on the list. "And?"

"And I took the bag out of his hands. He grabbed a handful of my hair, so I clobbered him. Not real hard, just enough to get him off of me."

"Anything else?"

She wrinkled a freckled nose thoughtfully. "He climbs a tree pretty good for an old guy."

"So it would seem," he said, stifling a smile.

Bobby turned to look at him. "I don't want to get in the way of what you have to do, but I won't let him drown this cat."

There was dead-on determination in her eyes. "Just sit tight for a minute." He headed over to the man Nathan had just talked down out of the tree.

Vern was a large rectangular man with a deeply lined face and wispy hair. "Well?" he demanded. "I don't see any handcuffs here. What are you waiting for? I want her arrested, and I want it done now. Bad enough I had to chase some gang off my property last night. Now I got to defend myself in the daytime."

"I think you need to calm down, Mr. Rosario. Back up a minute. Who was here last night?"

"How should I know who they were? Bunch of men and one woman, tramping around my property in the night."

"Where?"

Vern stabbed a finger eastward. "There. On the plot I'm clearing out this summer. I fired a shot and told them to get lost, whoever they were. Now today I got to deal with that girl."

"She offered to take the cat, Vern. Why didn't you let her?"

"I don't have to answer to anyone what I do with my property," he shouted around Jack's shoulder to the woman. "Not to no gang, and definitely not to no woman."

"You could have just given the cat to her and been done with it." Jack wanted to add, "you arrogant blowhard," but he restrained himself.

Vern suddenly pushed past Jack and strode toward Bobby. "I can do whatever I jolly well please with that cat," he said, spittle flying. "As a matter of fact, as soon as your scrawny carcass gets taken to the tank, I think I'm going to bash it a couple of times with a shovel before I throw it in the pond!"

She sprang from the rock and knocked the man to the ground, expertly flopping him over and planting her knee between his shoulder blades. She grabbed an ear with each hand and smashed his head into the ground. "You—will—not—kill—that—*cat*!" She punctuated each word with a smash.

Jack grabbed her around the waist and lifted her off of Vern, pulling her arms together behind her back. Nathan restrained the now-upright rancher.

"You see? Did you see that crazy broad attack me?" Vern screamed. "Put her away. Take her to the station and throw her in the clink."

Jack frog-marched Bobby several yards away and stood behind her, pinioning her arms until her breathing slowed. He spoke soothingly into her ear. "Okay, okay. Calm down. You need to get it together. Take a deep breath." He turned her around to face him. "Are you in control?"

She gazed past him, nostrils flared. "I will not let him kill that animal," she hissed through gritted teeth. "If you need to arrest me, go ahead, but I'm not leaving him with the cat."

"I know. I need you to let me handle it. Will you trust me to do that?" He gently tipped her chin so she had to look at him.

After a minute, she nodded.

"Stay here," he commanded. "Do not move from this spot."

He returned to the two men. "Okay, Mr. Rosario. Here's what you're going to do. You are going to let the lady have the cat, and we will remove them both from your property. No charges will be filed."

The man stared incredulously. "What? Are you insane? Why would I do that? I am the victim here."

"Because," he said, leaning forward until his face was very close to the other man's, "if you don't, I am going to tell every one of your bowling buddies that a woman the size of Minnie Mouse chased you up a tree and then kicked your sorry behind into the dirt."

Vern's eyes narrowed into vicious slits. "You can't do that."

"I sure as shootin' can. Now go back into your house and forget this ever happened."

Jack watched as the man grudgingly plodded back toward the house. Vern hesitated, and Jack added,

"Hey, Vern? I think Ellen Foots is going to get a little tip about animal cruelty at this address. She might want to check things out."

The man groaned and stalked into the house.

Bobby walked to the car, cradling the cat. "Who is Ellen Foots?"

"The Finny librarian and an amateur animal protection officer. She's six foot six inches of tempered steel without a shred of humor."

"I think I'd like to meet her."

He glanced at her and shuddered at the thought. "Get in the car, Bobby."

The ride back from Vern's was a very quiet one. Jack did not know quite what to say to the puzzling woman beside him. Bobby sat with the cat in her lap and watched the fog roll in over the top of Finny's Nose.

"Are those Douglas firs there?" she asked, squinting through the side window. "Just over the top of the nose? See that really big one right next to the smaller group?"

"You'll need to ask someone else, I'm afraid. I wouldn't know a Douglas fir from a Christmas tree," he said.

Bobby laughed. "They are Christmas trees. I just wondered how they got up there." She looked over at him. "Vern really shouldn't cut down that stand of trees. It's a crime to cut old-growth redwoods."

"It's his land. He can do what he wants." He cleared

his throat. "Bobby, you don't happen to be the woman Vern saw on his property last night, do you?"

"No, I reserve all my law breaking for the daylight hours."

"Good," he said with relief then suddenly checked his watch. "Uh-oh. I just realized what time it is. I promised Louella under pain of losing important parts of myself that I would be home by six sharp." He checked his watch again. "Five minutes to six. Would you be okay coming to my house for a minute before I take you home?"

She regarded him with the head-tilted glance. "Sure. Uncle Monk told me about Paul. Said he's a great kid. I'd love to meet him."

He nodded, swallowing hard. Visitors to the Denny household had been reduced to a trickle since Lacey died, except for an occasional colleague. He couldn't remember the last time he had invited someone into the house who wasn't wearing a badge. It might have been the cable guy.

They drove up to the small ranch-style home and pulled in along the street. Jack had not been able to park in the driveway next to the mailbox where Lacey died. Even now he waited until dark to retrieve the mail, whistling vigorously to prevent his mind from straying too far back to the past.

"I think maybe you ought to put your cat friend in the garage. I'm not sure Mr. Boo Boo will take to him."

Louella was waiting for them at the door. He introduced the two women. Louella didn't hide the surprise on her round face as she eagerly grasped

Bobby's hands and patted them. "Well, isn't it just a pleasure to meet you?" She beamed as she tucked flyaway strands of white hair behind her ears. "It's been an age since we've had company." She narrowed her eyes at Jack. "How come you didn't phone me to say you were bringing a visitor? I could have cooked something for you."

"It just sort of came up, Louella," he muttered. "Don't let us make you late for your meeting. Let me carry your bag to the car." He grabbed her canvas tote and headed to the front door.

"And this is Paul," Louella said. She stroked the blond hair of the boy who had suddenly materialized behind her leg.

The boy peeked around her ample flowered hip. "He's a good boy, so handsome and kind." She added slyly, "Just like his father."

He walked Louella to her car while she peppered him with questions about Cootchie and then Bobby. After he finally stowed her safely in the front seat, Jack returned to the house to find the front hallway empty. Following the sound of murmuring voices, he wandered into the family room.

He stopped dead in his tracks.

Bobby was lying on her stomach on the carpet, concentrating on a colorful pile of LEGOs. Paul was draped over her back, chin on top of her head, watching in breathless wonder.

He expected his son to hide in his room, or at the most ignore the guest as he typically did new people. "Wow," was all he could manage.

They both looked up. "It's better than wow. It's a rocket ship," Bobby said. "I'm a whiz at LEGOs, don't you think, Paul?"

The child nodded and rolled off of her to go search for his astronaut action figures.

She stood up. "Louella is nice. I get the feeling she thinks it's about time you brought a girl home."

He blushed and raked his fingers through his close-cropped hair. "Uh, yeah. I'm sorry she kind of put you on the spot."

"Not a problem," she said, walking to the back door and looking out into the yard.

A huge shadowy blur hurled itself against the sliding door. She leaped backward.

"Sorry. That's Mr. Boo Boo. He only knows a few tricks, and polite greetings are not one of them."

She looked at the dog with his tongue lolling out, one ear standing up and the other at right angles to it. "Does he have two different-colored eyes?"

"Yup. I think he was sort of assembled from leftover parts." He looked around distractedly, trying to remember how to engineer polite conversation.

"Hey, if I'm intruding here, I'll just head for home," she said.

"No, no." Suddenly he wanted her to stay, to keep standing there, looking at him from under the fringe of black hair that fell into her eyes. "I'm going to make Paul some dinner. Why don't you join us?"

"It might be less complicated if I didn't."

"How's that?"

"I'm a vegetarian."

He looked at her blankly. "A vegetarian?"

"Mm-hmm. You know, no meat."

"No meat?" he repeated.

"No meat. Chicken, beef, nothing that had a face. Maybe I'd better go home. Uncle Monk is used to my strange eating habits."

"No. No problem. Nothing with a face." Jack went to the kitchen and studied the contents of the fridge. Leftover meat loaf, Louella's. One chicken pot pie, Louella's. Some macaroni and cheese. Mustard. Black olives. Finger Jell-O. Eggs. He grabbed the egg carton and removed one. Eggs didn't have faces, he thought triumphantly. But they came from animals with faces. Hostile faces with beady yellow eyes and sharp beaks like Ruth's cranky birds, he remembered.

Bobby poked her head into the kitchen and startled him from his confused remunerations. "Jack?"

He whirled to face her, egg still in hand. "Yeah?"

"Eggs will work."

"Eggs will work," he repeated. "Okay then."

Thirty minutes later he had produced two pretty decent cheese omelets and sliced some ripe tomatoes from Louella's garden. Paul's plate was piled high with scrambled eggs and finger Jell-O.

The kitchen echoed with the sounds of Bobby's laughter and Paul blowing bubbles in his milk. After dinner, the boy sat down with a Thomas the Train video while Bobby helped clean up.

There was an intimacy in cleaning dishes together. Washing away the remnants of a shared meal. Drying the dishes and disclosing their secret resting places in the cupboard. Standing side by side in front of a chipped porcelain sink. It made him feel uneasy and foolishly pleased at the same time.

"So how are all your investigations going? Aren't you up to three now? Toes, Cootchie, and Ed Honeysill?"

"We're busy, all right. Things are going slowly, but the FBI is helping out with the Dent kidnapping."

"Thank God she's all right."

"I'll second that. I know you won't believe this, but life in Finny is generally quiet and uneventful." He thought about the strange path his day had taken since the call from Nathan summoning him to the Rosario farm. He smiled.

"What's funny?"

"Oh, I was just recalling the look on Vern's face after you steamrolled him."

"I only steamrolled him a little. You do think he deserved it, don't you?"

"Absolutely. I didn't think I'd ever meet the person who could put him in his place, though. You are the most fearless woman I have ever met."

She frowned, rubbing a dish. "I don't think I would describe myself as fearless."

"No? In the short time I've known you, you've trounced a guy in the bar and treed a cranky old codger who outweighs you by about one hundred fifty pounds. And you didn't even flinch at meeting my four-year-old. That isn't fearless?"

"I've been plenty afraid in my life. Everyone has fears, don't they?" She looked at her reflection in the ceramic dish. "When I was sixteen my mother got ovarian cancer. I was terrified that she would die. I skipped school constantly to stay home with her. I kept a four-leaf clover inside my bra and slept in the hallway outside her door for months, I was so afraid of losing her. I prayed until my fingers were numb. You know what?" Bobby put the dish into the cupboard. "She died anyway. I guess I just figured then that fear doesn't really change things much."

He nodded, remembering how the bottom had fallen out of his stomach when he got the phone call about Lacey. "But it sure is something you remember."

She looked at him closely. "Are you thinking about your wife?"

"Yes." He continued rinsing the omelet pan as he spoke. "It never occurred to me that I should worry about losing her. I never even entertained a thought about her dying until I got the call that she was gone. She died of a brain hemorrhage on her way to get the mail."

"That's when Paul stopped talking?"

"Yeah. He saw her die, I think. He didn't say a single word for two years." He closed his eyes to shut the pain back into place.

"How did you cope with it all?"

"Not very well. Day by day, like we're coping now. Lots of people helped out as much as they could, like Louella and Ruth. I get down on my knees and thank God for them every day. Things are better now that Paul is talking some."

He exhaled with a groan. "Now what really scares me is that he will forget his mother ever existed." The water gurgled quietly as is trickled down the drain. "I still can't really accept it. People tell me that God wouldn't give me more than I can bear, so I guess I need to toughen up."

She fished the rest of the silverware from the dregs of soapy water. "In my expert opinion, Jack your conclusion is a bit off."

His eyebrows shot up. "What?"

"Of course God gives us more than we, alone, can bear. Who can bear losing a wife while a child watches? Who can bear having a child kidnapped, for that matter? What about the parents who never get their kids back? No one can bear that, not alone. So He gives us people to lean on. People who shoulder the load when we can't do it one more minute." She looked him straight in the eye. "He gives us the miracle of a life and the tools to deal with all the junk that comes up in the course of living it."

He looked into her eyes, seeing the glimmer of earnestness that was so very rare in his experience. "You are unlike anyone I've ever known," he said softly.

Bobby chuckled and finished putting the silverware away. She peeked into the family room, where Paul slept in his train pajamas in front of the television.

"I've got to get going. Thanks for dinner, and tell Paul I want to show him how to make a LEGO space shuttle sometime. It will knock his socks off."

"Just a minute and I'll pop him into the car and drive you to the hotel."

"Don't bother. It's not far, and I like to walk at night." She noted the look of concern that stole across his face. "I think we've established that I can take care of myself."

"I know that, but I'd feel better if I took you home."

"I'll be fine." She picked up the box he'd found for her and headed to the garage to fetch the cat. "Besides, this is Finny. What could possibly happen?"

Ruth put her back into whipping cookie dough batter within an inch of its life. The muffins she'd made were already baked and cooled. Now she tossed handfuls of pecans and chocolate chips into the vanquished cookie dough.

Monk sat in a chair with a cup of coffee in one hand and a cookie in the other. "Ruth," he said between bites. "We're going to have to talk about this sometime."

"Talk about what?"

"You know what. You're avoiding the issue. You are upset about what happened to Cootchie, and I think you need to talk about it some more." There were lines of frustration on his face. "I love you. Let me help you with this."

"I am not avoiding the issue," she said. She added a teaspoon of vanilla. "I have to get these things baked for the sale tomorrow. Why do you say I'm avoiding the issue?"

"Because every time I try to talk to you about it, you bake another batch of cookies. So far you've made oatmeal raisin, snickerdoodles, and now chocolate chip."

"Chocolate pecan chunk."

"I stand corrected." He put the coffee down and stood, trying to catch her eye.

"I don't want to talk about anything." She couldn't understand the anger in her own voice. She wanted to wake up and find the whole mess over, forgotten, her carelessness erased like chalk from a blackboard. "I've got lots to do. It's the last festival weekend, and you know how Maude is."

"Okay. I can see this isn't going to get us anywhere." He rubbed his forehead above his massive eyebrows. "I'm new to this marriage stuff, Ruth. Plus I'm an old guy and I never got a chance to practice on anyone. I just want to say again that I love you and anytime you want to talk, I'm here."

She didn't know what to say. She knew she was being unfair to him, but she didn't know how to cope with his kindness on top of her own emotional maelstrom. It was a relief when the phone rang. "Yes?" she answered with a tremor in her voice. "Sure, Dimple. Okay. I can meet you there." She hung up. "I've got to go now."

She didn't dare to look at Monk's face as she took off her apron and scurried out the door.

Her feet took her to the door of the bungalow, though her mind screamed a protest every inch of the way. How could she face Dimple? What would she see in the woman's eyes? Anger? Disgust? Hatred, even? She knew it could not be put off for one more minute.

Her hand trembled as she knocked.

Dimple opened the door. She looked well, Ruth thought. There was color in her cheeks, and her eyes had lost their halos of misery.

"Hello, Ruth. Please come in. I have been thinking about you," she said.

She stepped through the door and stood facing the woman. Her whole body began to shake. "Dimple," she began, "how can I ever tell you how sorry I am? How terribly, terribly sorry I am?" She was terrified to see a look of recrimination on the young woman's face.

Dimple stopped her with a hug. "You have always been a blessing to me and my daughter. We love you just as we always have."

Ruth clung to her for a moment, until she noticed the objects stacked on the coffee table over Dimple's shoulder. "What are the suitcases for?" The question gave her mouth something to do, though she already knew the answer.

Dimple looked at her with somber green eyes. "I am going to send Cootchie to be with my—with Meg for a while. She has a big place in Phoenix and lots of room for Cootchie to run. I'll go visit them in a few days when I can get away." She squeezed Ruth's shoulder. "I just think it would be safer, until the villain is caught. It won't be for long, I promise."

Ruth nodded. She knew speaking would result in a torrent of tears. Already a chilling pain was mounting in the pit of her stomach, as though she had swallowed a frozen lump of granite.

"I'll go get her. She'll want to say good-bye." Dimple glided off toward the back of the house.

Slumped on the sofa, Ruth bit down hard on her index finger to keep from screaming aloud. She felt a weight on the couch next to her. Meg sat there in a fetching coral pantsuit. Tiny luminescent pearls dotted her earlobes, and her lipstick matched her outfit to a tee.

"I'd like to apologize for the things I said to you after Cootchie disappeared." She looked into Ruth's eyes. "I was upset, but that was no excuse to blame you for what happened." She took hold of her hands. "The fact of the matter is, you have taken excellent care of my daughter and granddaughter when I didn't have the courage to. I am in your debt, and I hope you can forgive me for what I said that day. I can only say again how truly sorry I am."

Ruth looked down at their clasped hands. Meg's skin was soft and unwrinkled. The fingernails were filed in graceful crescents and painted with a subtle creamy taupe. Her own hands were calloused, rough from dishwashing, and the nails were chewed off. She withdrew them from Meg's grasp.

"There's nothing to forgive. You didn't say anything out loud that I wasn't saying to myself. I won't ever forgive myself for what happened."

Meg was about to respond when Cootchie bounded into the room and jumped into Ruth's lap.

"Hi, Nana. I am goin' on a plane tomorrow," she said.

Ruth cleared her throat. "Yes, I heard you were going to stay with, ah, your grandma. That will be fun, won't it?"

"Yes, Nana." The girl played with the strings on Ruth's sweat jacket.

She smoothed the girl's flyaway curls, savoring the silkiness with her fingertips.

"Cootchie, Nana is very sorry. I should have been watching you more closely. So the—the man couldn't have taken you. Nana made a terrible mistake." The words burned her mouth.

Cootchie fixed her heavily lashed eyes on Ruth. "It's okay, Nana. I went to de library. I got a book on rocks. When I come back, we can hunt for rocks together. Okay?"

Ruth could not answer. She hugged Cootchie and buried her face in the mounds of curly hair. "I love you, Cootchie," she whispered. "I love you."

"I love you, too, Nana." Cootchie danced away to find her magnifying glass to add to the collection of things in her suitcase.

Somehow Ruth made her way to the door and said her good-byes to Dimple and Meg. The door closed behind her, and she staggered down the walkway to the trees at the end of the drive.

Monk stood there with his hands in his pockets. "I thought maybe you could use a shoulder."

Ruth began to cry bitter tears. He folded her in his arms and held her.

⁓

Maude called almost hourly to add more afternoon Mrs. Fog appearances for the final weekend of the festival. Ruth appreciated Maude's intention—to keep her mind and heart busy. Monk plied her constantly with containers of soup and homemade bread.

She was in a fog, shrouded by the horrible "what

if" feelings that swirled inside her head. As much as she struggled against it, she felt herself sliding back into the black depression that had gripped her soul after her first husband's death. She'd lived in that darkness for years, but since she'd started her new life with Monk, it had disappeared. Now it was back with a vengeance.

A steely resolve crept up inside her. No. She would not allow the darkness to overtake her again. She had fought too hard, too long to let it take away her soul a second time. She gripped her hands together and prayed until her fingers were numb.

When she opened her eyes, she was filled with a need to do something. Anything. In a blink, she knew where she had to go. If Monk was right and God gave her courage because He knew she would use it, then it was time to face her demons. Maybe there was something there, some infinitesimal clue that would reveal who had taken Cootchie on that terrible day. It was all she could think to do.

Monk offered to accompany her up nose, but Ruth knew she had to do it alone. At least, almost alone. She took an eager Martha along with her for feathery moral support. The bird felt warm against her chest, soft feathers silky under her chin.

As she passed the Buns Up Bakery, she noticed a familiar face. It was Candace, sitting at a corner table, talking on her cell phone. Judging from the woman's expression, it was not a pleasant conversation. Suffering from an acute case of nosiness and procrastination, Ruth walked inside the store, tucking Martha into her jacket.

The delectable smell of apple fritters filled the small space.

Al, the owner, greeted her cheerfully. "Ruth. It's so great, isn't it? Cootchie is back and no worse for the wear."

Ruth nodded, unable to find words for a moment.

Al continued to ramble on as Ruth eavesdropped on Candace's conversation in the corner.

"I don't think so," Candace muttered. "Nothing has changed."

Al put two fritters in a bag. "I been thinking about that toe. Where do you think it came from?" he asked. "Do you think it is related to the kidnapping or to Honeysill's murder?"

Ruth shot a quick glance at Candace. "I don't know." Ruth took the bag and paid for the treats. "It's a mystery to me."

He leaned toward her. "Plenty of strangers in town. Some of them up to no good. I saw a guy in here yesterday. He talked like a New Yorker. Wore real fancy clothes and all."

"Who was he with?"

"He came in alone, but then he struck up quite a conversation with that balloon guy." Al wiped down the counter as he whispered. "Ask Hugh. He was here. He can tell you about it."

She thanked Al and turned to leave just as Candace finished her conversation.

"No. That's it. I don't have anything else to say to you."

She punched off the phone and met Ruth at the door.

"Hello, Candace. How are you holding up?" Now that the woman was close, Ruth could see the lines etched into her dusky skin.

"I am okay, but I can't wait to leave this town."

Ruth nodded. "I can imagine there aren't many good memories for you here." Martha poked her head out of the jacket to peck at the paper bag.

"I've got to stay until the end of the week," Candace said. "The insurance company is sending someone out, so I've got to answer more questions." Her eyes were dull.

"Oh?" She pulled the bag out of the bird's beak.

"Ed had a pretty substantial life insurance policy, and I'm the beneficiary, so I guess that makes me look pretty suspicious."

Ruth wondered if Bing had known about the policy before the crash, but she didn't dare ask.

Candace said good-bye.

"All right, Martha," she said. "Let's get this over with." Without a word to anyone else, she headed up nose.

It took her a very long time to reach the spot where Cootchie had disappeared and a very short time to pass through it. As she approached the horribly familiar ground, Ruth felt herself in the grip of a terrible guilt; a feeling that somehow she had changed things forever with one moment of carelessness.

There was nothing here to fill in the blanks, no answers lying in the weeds, just trampled grass and a rotten log.

Cootchie was gone with Meg. When and if Cootchie and Dimple returned, Ruth was not sure they would slip back into the easy life they enjoyed before. She didn't know if Dimple could ever trust her fully again. She wasn't sure she would ever trust herself.

"Oh God, please help me." She wanted to ask for forgiveness again. To ask Him to take away the curiosity that distracted her from her duty that day. For the strength to face what could have happened. The words would not come out. He had already forgiven her anyway, she knew. She had to find a way to forgive herself.

She had to do something, anything to help Dimple, to make amends. There were the daily chores at Dimple's farm that needed doing and had no doubt been neglected for days. The thoughts churned through her mind faster and faster until her feet picked up the frenzy. She scooped up the tern, who squawked in protest, and began running. She didn't stop until she staggered across the threshold of the Pistol Bang Mushroom Farm.

The place was as lush as ever, she noticed through the searing cramp in her side. It seemed to have a Brigadoonesque ability to thrive no matter what wintry blight the world outside was struggling with. As she deposited a writhing Martha on the ground, Ruth was surprised to see Hugh exiting the polytunnel.

"I didn't expect to see you here."

The young man looked up abruptly. "Oh, hi, Ruth. I came by to check on the shiitakes. They are pretty close to harvesting. Do you think Dimple will be back soon? I can handle the harvest if she isn't. I know the ropes."

"I can't really say. Why don't you give her a call? I'm sure she would appreciate talking to you."

Hugh became engrossed in his boots. "Oh, I don't want to bug her or anything. She's really had it rough lately."

She felt her heart give a painful twist. "Yes, she has, I'm afraid."

"Cootchie is all right, isn't she?"

"She handled the whole thing better than all of us."

"It turned out okay, then. Lucky for everyone."

Ah, the wonderful optimism of youth. "I thought I would check the office while I'm here."

"Yeah. Good idea. I gotta go. If you see Dimple, tell her, uh, I'll be talking to her soon, okay?"

"Okay." He plodded down the gravel walkway like a stork waddling through a muddy marsh.

Ruth spent the next hour emptying wastebaskets, sweeping the office floor, and taking messages off the answering machine. Typically Ruth did these chores for Dimple on a weekly basis, but now the duties seemed imbued with a new importance. When she could think of nothing else to do, she locked up and walked into the garden.

She felt exhausted. As much as she wanted to collapse on the wooden bench, she knew if she didn't get home in a timely fashion, Monk would come puffing up nose to find her.

As she heaved herself downslope, Martha in tow, a small figure approached. She recognized Bobby, pink cheeked, consulting a piece of paper taken from her denim jacket.

"Hi. Where are you headed?"

"Hey, Ruth." She closed the gap between them and bent to scratch Martha's head. "I'm off to the top of Finny's Nose. I want to check something out. How are you doing? I haven't seen you in the coffee shop." She brushed dark hair out of her eyes. "Uncle Monk said you've been kind of down about everything."

"I'm trying to hold myself together. It's been hard." She was dismayed to feel tears stinging her eyes. "To think what could have happened."

"Could haves can kill you."

Ruth looked at her curiously. "You sound like you have some experience with catastrophes."

She laughed. "Hasn't everyone? By the way, Ruth, is Finny's Nose private or public property?"

"It belonged to the Dent family for many generations, but Buster gave it to the city to keep in preserve. I guess you'd call it a regional open space."

"Hmm." Bobby's brow furrowed. "Okay, thanks. I've gotta get going before I lose the daylight. I want to drag Jack up here to show him something, and I need to do my homework."

"Jack? Jack Denny? He doesn't seem like the nature-loving type."

"He isn't. Hence the verb 'drag.' "

"What do you think about these mysterious people parading around at night?"

"I think they're ecoterrorists."

"I read something about that on the Internet. I can't believe people would go to such lengths to further a cause."

"They believe they have a moral imperative to protect the earth," Bobby said, "even if it means breaking the law."

Ruth thought about Rocky's earlier comment. *"We'll be gone before anyone is the wiser."*

"What does Jack think about that?" she asked.

"I haven't gotten that far with him. We've been working on other issues."

Ruth was secretly thrilled to imagine Jack spending time with this interesting young woman. As far as she knew, he hadn't seen anyone since Lacey died.

"I have forgotten how long Monk said you were staying in town," Ruth said. The Fog Festival would be finished in the next two days. She was hoping the girl was planning to hang around for a while after the festival limped to a close. It would give Jack a little more time with her.

"I'm here at least through the festival. The park I work at has closed for flood cleanup for two months, so I've got some time. Maybe if Uncle Monk is still really busy, I'll hang out here for a few more months."

Ruth made a mental note to inform Monk that he needed to be very busy for the next few months.

"Are you going to make it home all right? You look tired."

"Oh sure. I've got my attack bird here to look out for me."

They both looked at Martha, who sat on the ground at Ruth's feet. The slender bird had closed her tiny eyes and tucked her beak into her downy chest. "Yup. I'm sure no one will pester you with that critter on duty. See you later."

The young woman walked briskly upslope, leaving Ruth to wonder what sort of homework could be done by a determined woman all alone at the top of a mountain.

⌁

That night Ruth could not sleep, even after her sprint up to the mushroom farm. Perhaps it was the lingering terror from the abduction, or the emotional discussion with Dimple, or the persistent heartburn that nagged her stomach. Maybe it was just the continuing trauma of knowing that Cootchie was in Arizona that kept Ruth wide awake at one forty-five on Sunday morning. Determined not to watch the hands of her bedside clock tick off another hour, she wrapped herself in a worn flannel robe, slid quietly out of bed without disturbing Monk, and retreated to her place of refuge. The kitchen.

She knew the best thing for crisis control was chocolate, but for some reason she could not drum up an appetite for it. Even the piles of plastic-wrapped cookies on the counter did not tempt her.

Everything had been going so well. Her small family, weird though it was, was happy and content. Then it had all gone directly downhill. Ed's murder, Meg Sooner's arrival, Cootchie's kidnapping. And the strain the whole event had put on her new marriage. She loved Monk without reservation, but this was the first real trauma in their relationship. Was it the brevity of their marriage or the fact that she had weathered many crises alone that kept her from fully unburdening herself to him? She had never entertained the foggiest notion of relating to anyone of the male species after her husband died. Firmly she propelled the thoughts from her head. She had gotten past that hurdle, and she would get through this one, too, with God's help. It was time to start using the strength He gave her to face problems, relationship or otherwise, head-on.

A metallic crash from outside made her jump.

Her heart beat wildly as she turned on the porch light and squinted into the backyard. The weak light picked up millions of tiny water droplets, thick as snow. It did not illuminate anything else.

Rats, she thought, *the birds have probably gotten out again.* She put a hand on the dead bolt and stopped.

A ripple of terror crept through her, as if some part of her mind could see farther into the darkened yard.

And what it saw scared her.

She pulled her hand away from the locked door and cried out.

Monk got downstairs in a flash. He was wearing a frayed sweat suit emblazoned with the word *Navy*. There was a baseball bat in his hand. His eyes were still sleep glazed. "I heard you call out my name, or did I dream that?"

"I'm sorry. Maybe I'm just being dramatic," she said, her cheeks warm. "There might be nothing out there. My imagination has been in overdrive these past few days."

"You did the right thing. I'm not sure if an old chef like me can protect you from anything other than a marauding head of garlic, but I'll give it my able best."

She handed him a flashlight.

A blast of cold air hit them both as Monk opened the sliding door. "Stay here and keep the phone handy." He vanished into the fog.

Several minutes later he was back. "Well, the birds are still penned and safe. There's nothing that I can see out of order, although your side gate is unlatched. Any chance you left it open?"

She shook her head. "I always double-check at night in case the birds make it over the wall. It was definitely closed before."

They looked at each other for a minute. "Come outside with me. Maybe you'll notice something that I didn't."

She checked first on the birds to reassure herself of their well-being, though she needn't have bothered. Seven pairs of yellow eyes glared balefully at her from behind their chain link enclosure. They had the "You'd better be carrying a bag of Fritos" look on their hostile faces. Her flashlight illuminated the rest of the area a slice at a time.

It took her two passes around the yard before she noticed.

"I can't believe it," she said.

"What?"

"My castings. Three buckets of worm castings for Royland. They were right here on the porch. They're gone."

"Worm castings." Monk shook his head in confusion. "Doesn't seem like they are worth the trouble."

"Not really. Twenty dollars apiece, unless you have to spring for the eighteen-dollar shipping and handling fee."

"Let's go back in and see if we can unmuddle this mess."

Safely inside with mugs of hot decaf coffee, they plopped down on the sofa.

"Why would someone want your castings?"

Ruth couldn't see why someone would want to steal them. They were the by-product of the worm after it swallowed soil and plant litter. The material mixed in the digestive tract and came out as casts. "As far as I know, it's only used by organic farmers as a fertilizer. That's what Royland uses it for. Some florists use it for ornamental plants grown in baskets, I suppose."

"I can't picture a nefarious florist heisting your castings in the dead of night," he said thoughtfully.

"Me neither. Maybe someone mistook the buckets for something else."

"Were they labeled?"

"Just with the Phillip's Worm Emporium sticker on them."

They mulled it over for an hour more before he carried his mug to the sink. "I'm going to sleep down here tonight. Just in case whoever it was comes back." He looked at her open mouth. "If anything is going to come through that door, it will have to get by this old battleship."

"Thank you." She swallowed the emotion rising in her throat. "I'm sorry I've been acting strange lately." Her eyes glistened with tears. "I love you."

16

At half past 2:00 a.m. on Saturday, Jack was driving down the dark frontage road after checking the parking lot where most of the festival vendor trailers were situated. All was quiet on the western front. God willing, it would stay that way for the last two days of the festival craziness. He had enough ongoing investigations to last for months.

A light drizzle speckled his windshield, and he turned up the heater to fight off the wet chill. Finny was closed up tight, like a vacuum-sealed jar. The only place open for business was Eden Hospital. It crossed his mind to stop there to see if they could give him an IV coffee drip.

Maybe he could get Alva to take a look at the evil Mr. Coffee. If he promised him a bag of jelly beans, the old man would do it. If he threw in some candy corns, Alva would no doubt have a crack at the ancient pencil sharpener, too. Jack was trying to figure out how early was too early to call on Alva when he noticed a slender woman walking along the shoulder, hunched inside a waterproof jacket. Pulling up alongside the pedestrian, he rolled down his window.

"Isn't it kind of late for a walk?" he asked.

"A little early, I'd say." Bobby stuck her head in his passenger window. "I'm involved in an investigation. Don't hassle me, copper."

He laughed. "Why don't you get in and tell me about it?"

She hopped into the car and wiped the moisture from her face. "Okay, but don't go blabbing it around. I'm investigating some strange doings up nose."

"Really?"

"Really. Drive to the trailhead and I'll show you."

He looked into her brown eyes, and for a split second he would have rolled himself in bacon grease and walked into a lion's den if she suggested it. Mentally he shook himself back to the rational world. "Let's go."

After a mile he pulled off the main road and they got out of the car. The rain had stopped, and the moon shone between the clouds.

"Look," she commanded, pointing up nose.

Jack squinted. "I don't see anything but the end of your finger."

"Come on, Detective. Be patient and keep looking."

Then he saw it.

A pocket of light flickered unsteadily halfway up the steep wooded hill. "Huh. I wonder what in the world is going on up there."

"That's exactly what I was going to find out."

"Alone? In the dark? After all the murder and mayhem that's been going on around here?"

Her lips curled in a crooked smile. "What's the matter? You don't think I can handle it?"

"Oh, I'm fairly certain you can handle anything. Why don't I come along anyway and you can protect me?" He waited for her nod and contacted the police dispatcher to fill her in on his plans. He grabbed his radio and clipped it to his belt.

"Onward and upward," he said.

They walked easily for the first mile. The slope was mild and speckled with enough trees to screen them from whatever was at the top. The full moon shone just enough for them to pick their way up the uneven trail. When Bobby stumbled, he instinctively reached an arm around her waist to steady her. He found her scent tantalizing.

"Are you sniffing me?"

Jack felt his face warm, and he was grateful for the darkness. "Uh, well, actually. . . Sorry about that. I think my brain is scrambled, but you smell just like a strong cup of French roast coffee." He felt like an idiot for saying the words out loud.

Her laugh echoed softly. "I think I did splash a little on my shirt during my shift at Uncle Monk's. I take it your coffee machine is still on the fritz?"

"Yup," he said. "We're getting close to declaring a national emergency."

"So next time I'm out scouting for a man, I'll pass up the Chanel No. 5 and rub some coffee grounds on my wrists." She tucked dark hair behind her ears.

"That would definitely get my attention."

They lapsed into silence as the slope became steeper. Their breath came out as white puffs in the cold air. They stopped now and then to look up at the moon. It was round and full as a ripe melon. As he began to pant, he noticed Bobby's breathing was not labored in the slightest. "So how do you like the park ranger gig? Better than bus driver?"

"Definitely. I started out as an interpreter, leading

tours and stuff like that. It was fun, but the real excitement started when I got into the law enforcement end of it." She stopped to shake a rock out of her boot. "It's still blows me away that I get to work in some of the most gorgeous places on earth, and I get paid for it."

"Sounds perfect."

"Not perfect. Wide-open spaces are very freeing to people. On the one hand, it lets them escape from the status stuff—cars, clothes, Starbucks. It kind of puts everyone on a level playing field. The downside is sometimes people misuse the freedom. Think they can get away from the rules that apply in the civilized world."

"What kind of stuff do you have to deal with?" He pushed aside a low-hanging branch.

"Drinking, drug use. Small-time, mostly, but sometimes it gets to be dicey when it's time to arrest someone. And in the past few years, we've got bigger problems. Drug rings starting up plantations on the outskirts of the park."

"I've heard about that. How do you handle it?'

"You pray you don't stumble into a crop when you're alone. And you really hope they aren't packing a bigger weapon than you are." Her teeth gleamed in the moonlight. "You can relate, I bet."

"Sure can." He could relate completely, and it astonished him. This woman was so different from Lacey, yet he connected with her easily. It was a connection that had been missing from his life for years.

She frowned. "You know, I saw Ed Honeysill headed

up here just before his balloon crashed. He said he was out for a walk, and I didn't question it at the time, but I wonder if I should have mentioned it before."

Jack tried to figure a reason other than exercise why Ed would climb up nose. He couldn't think of one.

As they neared the plateau at the top of Finny's Nose, they slowed their pace to avoid twigs and pockets of leaves. In the clearing just ahead, they could hear voices. Orange flames danced in the distance.

They came within several yards of the clearing before they crouched down behind some scrubby bushes.

Five figures, dressed in dark clothes with bandannas on their heads, sat in a circle. One of the group stood in the approximate center of the clearing bent over a campfire. The light caught her for a second, revealing a woman with long silvered hair. A pile of duffel bags and rope lay nearby, as well as a pile of metal rods.

"It's Evelyn Bippo," Bobby breathed in Jack's ear, sending tingles down his back. "I don't recognize the others."

"The tall one, there. I think that's Rocky. It looks like his ponytail hanging out, anyway," Jack said. "What are they saying?"

They strained to make out the words. "Somehow I don't think it's 'Rah rah ree, kick 'em in the knee.'" She giggled.

Without warning, one of the figures pulled a knife from his pocket.

Jack grunted as he reached to draw his gun.

"Wait," she whispered, squeezing his arm. "They're

not going to hurt him."

Rocky stood up and took the knife. He raised his voice to a near shout. "Today we recognize Dan as a member of the GOPs for his role in planning our next act of liberation." Then he turned the knife and presented it, handle first, to the man seated next to him.

More conversation followed, but it was too low for Jack to make out.

Bobby grabbed Jack's free hand and leaned close. "Let's go. I'll fill you in after we get out of here."

The sun was just beginning to pry feebly at the foggy night when they made it back to the car. Jack fired up the engine and cranked the heater to megablast. They bumped along until they reached the main road.

"All right. Let's have it," Jack said.

She clamped her teeth together to stop the chattering and looked at her watch. "Well, since it's almost morning, why don't you take me back to the coffee shop. I have a key. I'll make us some breakfast. I think I've got some 'splaining to do."

He couldn't have agreed more.

17

Ruth hung up the phone for the fifth time.

Monk sat bleary eyed at the kitchen table, coffee mug in hand.

"Just call her already," he said. "You're driving yourself nuts."

"I don't know. Maybe it's a bad idea. What if she doesn't want me to speak to her? What if she hangs up? Besides, it's really early."

"She won't hang up, and it's an hour ahead in Phoenix. That makes it a leisurely 8:05 there, and she's taking care of a three-year-old. We're talking Cootchie here. That woman has been up since the first beam of dawn."

He was right. Cootchie was always up before the roosters finished their cock-a-doodling. She greeted each morning as if it was made just for her and she didn't want to miss a minute. Ruth dialed with a trembling finger. She watched Monk as the phone rang for the third time. He sat there drinking coffee and eating chocolate chip cookies as if he had always belonged there as much as her ancient beloved blender.

"These are great, honey, really great," he said around a mouthful of cookie. "The perfect breakfast food. You should give me the recipe. No, never mind, you should make them for me on a regular basis. That's a better idea."

She smiled at him around the phone mouthpiece.

"I'll think about it. Oh no, someone is answering. What should I say? Hello, uh, Mrs. Sooner? Uh, it's me, Ruth. Ruth Budge. I hope I'm not calling too early. Uh, I wanted to call before the festival activities get under way."

He started on his second cup of coffee while she waited for the polite small talk to subside.

"Er, I was wondering. I've been missing Cootchie so much. I just was thinking maybe I could talk to her. That is, if you think it's okay. I know you just got settled in there and all, but I wanted to hear her voice. It's silly."

"I think that would be fine. Cootchie mentions you all the time," Meg said.

"Oh really?" Ruth tried to hide the ecstasy in her voice.

"Yes. She's also been saying things that I just don't understand. I think it's something to do with squirrels."

"Squirrels?" She laughed. "Well, you never really know what's going on in that brain."

"I certainly don't." Meg's voice dropped a notch. "She's been talking about the man who took her."

Ruth could feel her heart begin to pound with the force of a jackhammer. "What did she say? Is it anything that could be helpful to the police?"

"I'm not sure. Why don't you talk to her? Here she is."

There was a second delay while Meg handed the phone to Cootchie.

"Hi, Nana Ruth."

"H–hi, Cootchie." She fought the tears that suddenly flooded her eyes. "Are you having fun with your grandma?"

"Yes, Nana. We find rocks. I saw a rabbit with big ears but no squirrels here, Nana. De muffin man says good squirrels is dead squirrels."

"The muffin man?" Ruth gave Monk a baffled look. "Who is the muffin man?"

"De man who took me to de library. De muffin man."

"Uh, the muffin man, like the 'Do you know the muffin man?' rhyme?"

"What rhyme?"

She gave herself a mental whack. Of course Cootchie would have no idea about nursery rhymes. The child was more familiar with Molière than Mother Goose. "Never mind, Cootchie. The man, the muffin man. Did he stop at the store to get muffins when you, er, went to the library?"

"No, Nana. He grewed them."

"He grewed, grew them? He grew the muffins?"

"Yes. I have to go find rocks. Today I will dig a well to make wishes in. Good-bye. I love you, Nana."

Ruth whispered, "I love you, too," as the phone line went dead.

Monk insisted that a morning walk along the beach would be just the ticket for Ruth's dark mood. She was not sure that taking a flock of seven crabby gulls along was the ticket to anything but a bleeding ulcer, but it seemed like a good way to avoid the Saturday festival crowds. She thought that speaking to Cootchie would help ease her heart, but it seemed to stir up the emptiness even more.

The waves clawed angry foamy fingers against the gravel. The birds waddled in obvious bliss, poking around for bits of plants and unsuspecting pale crabs. A low-lying fog layer diminished as the birds watched, leaving only a cold wind behind. Maude would not be pleased.

Monk reached in between Teddy and Grover to separate them when they came to blows over a dropped pretzel that lay on the beach. "All right, you nasty critters," he said. "Enough of that squabbling. Did you bring anything to help round them up?"

She pointed at her pocket. "Fritos. Don't leave home without them."

He sidled closer and closer until he draped a huge arm over her shoulders.

"I need body heat," he said. "I'm freezing."

"I could remind you that it was your idea to come here," she said.

"It seemed like a sound, husbandly suggestion at the time."

A man in a jogging suit trotted into view. It was Bing Mitchell, with hardly a bead of sweat on his brow.

"Hey there. So the kid's been found," he called as he jogged up to them.

"Yes, she has," Ruth said. "How did you hear about it?"

"Hugh told me."

"She's just fine," Monk said. "Safe and sound."

"That's good. Say, I understand Hugh's old man is looking to unload some property. Have there been any offers made on it?"

"I really couldn't say," Ruth said. "You'll have to talk to Royland about that. Why do you ask?"

"Just looking to expand the business. Are you folks going to make the Fog Festival an annual thing?"

She exchanged a look with Monk.

"I sincerely hope not," she said.

"You really should think twice. It brings people here from all over."

Monk shot him a look. "Exactly," he said.

The young man laughed and stretched his arms in a wide arc. "I'd better get back to my run. See you soon." He ran on down the beach, passing another figure running in the opposite direction.

Alva careened awkwardly toward them, his knobby knees pasty white above striped crew socks.

"Hey," Monk said. "What are you doing? Bicycles are better for exercise than jogging, my man."

Alva staggered to a halt. He panted heavily and held the canvas fishing hat on his head with both hands. "I ain't exercising. I found it. I finally found it. Come on!" With that he turned his back on them and galloped back to the lichen covered boulders lying in reckless confusion several yards away.

Ruth and Monk looked at each other and followed him as fast as the shifting sand would allow. When they got to the rock pile, Alva stabbed a finger under the eroded side of the granite that made a shelf a few feet above the ground.

They ducked their heads to get a better look.

Ruth screamed and covered her hands with her mouth.

18

Not bad for a vegetarian," Jack said around a mouthful of blueberry pancakes.

"Just because I don't eat meat doesn't mean I can't cook," Bobby said. She took off her apron and walked around from behind the counter of Monk's Coffee and Catering. "Coffee?"

His smile was blissful. "I haven't had a good cup of coffee in—"

"Hours?"

"Feels like years." He noticed the way her hair curled from the wet hike down the hill, framing her flushed cheeks. He cleared his throat. "Okay, spill it. What's the deal with the knife people?"

She pushed the damp bangs out of her face. "I can't speak for all people, but this group looked a lot like some that descend on the national parks every time some deforesting needs to be done."

"Deforesting?"

"Yeah. Controlled burns, cutting to quarantine disease, that sort of stuff."

"Uh-huh. Does that have to be done often?"

"Thankfully, no. Certain strategic sites need to be thinned sometimes to control runaway wildfires. The gap in the understory, the plant growth under the big trees, creates kind of a speed bump that slows the fire. Some level of fire is good for the ecology. It burns off duff, the low-lying stuff on the ground, and clears the way for new growth."

"Makes sense."

"It's the runaway fires that are bad, and those happen most often in the dense areas. If you've got a real thick tree cover, it creates kind of a ladder effect."

She noted his furrowed brow. "Fire can climb from the ground to the treetops. Then the flares carry it from tree to tree when it's really windy. When you get crown fires like that, you're in trouble. They burn hot, fast, and high. Not much can stop them at that point."

He watched her while he sipped, admiring the play of early morning light on her face.

"Then there's the disease factor," she said. "In my park we have huge numbers of old-growth oaks. There have been years when we had a real problem with oak wilt, and the only way you can effectively control that is to clear out the sick trees before it spreads."

"I'm not clear on why people would oppose these techniques," he said between bites.

"No one likes to cut down a tree, especially not a park ranger," she said, fixing her intense black eyes on his, "but sometimes it is necessary to prevent a bigger loss. Most people don't have a problem with that, but there's a radical element that feels any tree cutting is wrong."

"And you think that's what we've got here, with Rocky Bippo and company? Have you ever heard of a group called the GOPs?"

"No, but I get the feeling the Bippos are involved in something along those lines. Traveling the festival circuit gives them an opportunity to visit plenty of different locales. The vending business provides a livelihood of sorts."

He took a swallow of coffee. "The sister seems to be legit with the dog thing."

"She probably is. I think most conservation groups have pure motives. It's when they become above the law that you've got a problem. Evelyn may be sucked into the whole thing because of her brother, too. You never know."

"He's a hothead."

Bobby ate a bite of pancake. "Last season we had to cut a stand of trees to prevent the spread of wilt, and we had protesters coming out of the woodwork, claiming it was being done for profit or some such thing. Most of the people were harmless enough, but there were five arrests out of that whole episode, and my partner got his jaw broken when his Jeep ran into a blockade they put on the trail."

Jack shook his head. "What's up with the knife?"

"I think it's some sort of hazing ritual. You're only a trusted member after you've plotted some sort of protest crime. It's easier to trust each other when you've all done something illegal together. Doesn't pay to squeal on a buddy when you'll go to the slammer right along with him."

"So Rocky and his gang are working on some mischief while they're here. Any guesses?"

"Remember the metal rods we saw? Next to the rope? I'm betting they're planning on spiking Vern's trees to make it impossible for him to chop them down." She smiled wickedly. "It's wrong, though I would enjoy seeing the look on his face when his plans went south."

"Me, too, but I'm going to have to put a damper on that scheme anyway. The Finny PD does not have the time or resources for any more investigations at the present time. We're full up."

Bobby refilled his mug and her own. "Who would think Finny could be such a hotbed of discontent?"

"Who indeed? At least I've got enough information to put a monkey wrench in the evil plan." He looked down at the pager on his belt. "I have to take a call."

Bobby poured more syrup on her pancake.

"Jack Denny," he said into the cell phone. After a minute his eyes widened, and he said, "I'm on my way."

"I've gotta go. That was Mary—she's on her way to the beach." He drained the coffee cup in one gulp. "It sounds like Alva finally found the body he's been looking for."

～

The sand-covered lump behind Alva was indeed a body. Idly Jack thought how disappointed Bobby was when she had to stay to open Monk's shop instead of accompanying him. He refocused on his duty.

Mary was already on scene, talking into her radio.

Jack could discern the denim-covered legs on one end with knees curled up close to the torso. One hand covered the face. The hand was coated with a layer of blood and grit.

"See?" Alva stage-whispered, his eyes popping. "I told ya there was a body around to go with that toe."

Jack felt slightly sheepish recalling the way he'd

dismissed Alva's ramblings after they'd failed to find any body to match the toe.

"All right. Stand back there with Ruth and Monk, okay?" He and Mary squatted gingerly beside the body, and Jack reached out two fingers to check the wrist for a pulse.

The body sat up.

Jack stood abruptly. Mary fell in the sand. Ruth, Monk, and Alva shouted simultaneously and leaped back.

The face that presented itself to them was covered in mud and grime. One of the eyes was swollen shut, and a wide smear of blood leaked from a grotesquely swollen upper lip. A pair of smashed glasses lay on the sand.

"Oh no! It's Hugh," Ruth gasped.

"Aw, gee, Detective," Alva said. "It ain't a dead body. Only a live one."

"That's okay, Alva. Better luck next time." He knelt next to Hugh. "Are you okay, son? The ambulance is on its way."

Hugh coughed and groaned.

"Monk, there's a bottle of water on the front seat of my car. Do you mind?" Jack said, handing him the keys.

" 'Course not." Monk lumbered off.

Ruth extracted a tissue from her pocket and tried to brush some of the dirt out of Hugh's eyes.

"Can you tell me what happened?" Jack asked.

He mumbled and coughed several more times. "Those gang people."

"Who?" Mary said.

"The bandanna gang. They were here on the beach early this morning." He began to groan again, holding his side.

"Oh my gosh," Ruth gasped. "I saw them, too, Sunday night."

Jack looked up sharply. "You told me about that, but you said you weren't sure they meant any harm. Did they threaten you directly?"

"They didn't say a word to me, I just ran as soon as I came upon them."

"Okay." Jack turned to the boy. "You were here at the beach this morning and you saw them? What time was that?"

"Around five. I woke up early and decided to take a walk. They were here. They saw me watching them, and they—" He squeezed his eyes shut. "They beat me up. They said they would kill me for spying on them."

Monk returned and handed over an opened water bottle to Hugh. "Well, you sure took a lickin' there, young fella," he said.

The fire chief and another firefighter arrived carrying a medical supply box. They knelt beside Hugh and began to check his pulse and pupils.

Jack looked over their shoulder. "Did you know any of your attackers, Hugh? Could you identify them?"

He shook his head. "I didn't see their faces. It was still dark."

"Could you recognize their voices?"

"No. It didn't sound like anyone I'd met before." He winced as Ernie prodded his ribs. "I just saw the bandannas."

"Can we have some space here, Detective?" Ernie said.

Jack, Ruth, and Monk moved away. Mary stayed with Ernie and snapped pictures of the crime scene. They watched as the firefighters bandaged various cuts and abrasions. Hugh stood unsteadily amid a shower of gravel.

"What's going on?" Jack asked. "He needs to go to the hospital."

"I know." Ernie removed his latex gloves with an annoyed snap. "You can lead an idiot to water, but you can't make him go to the hospital."

"Hugh," Ruth said, "you've got to go. I'm sure you've got broken ribs and maybe a concussion. It's best if you go to the hospital."

"No," he croaked. "I'll be fine. I just need a ride home."

Jack sighed. "How about I take you home and we'll talk more about who attacked you."

"No way," Hugh said, swiping at a trickle of blood under his eye. "Forget about the whole thing. There's no way I'm identifying anybody or pressing charges. I just want to go home." He stood and limped his way up the beach.

Jack took him home.

⁓

The officers ducked under the beaded curtain that served as a doorway to Rocky's booth at the edge of the field. Nate swatted at a blue crystal bead that clung to his hair. Waist-high wooden cases housed baskets of polished agate stones, tie-dyed shirts, and porcelain fairies. Dozens of tree ornaments made of metal, glass, and ceramic hung overhead. They twirled in the early morning breeze. A few stalwart shoppers meandered along the row of craft booths, but none had made it into Rocky's stall.

Rocky looked up from the box he was rummaging through. His long braid twisted over one shoulder. "What can I do for you?"

"Hello, Mr. Bippo," Jack said. "You remember Officer Katz. We'd like to talk with you for a minute."

Rocky regarded them through slitted eyes. "What about?"

"About an attack that happened last night."

"An attack?"

"Yes," Jack said, "a young man was beaten severely."

"Beaten?" Rocky whistled. "Wow, beatings, explosions, murder. This is a dangerous town."

"It seems to be getting that way," Nate chimed in.

"Yeah," Jack said. "What was that Alva was saying, Nate? Something about a gang on the beach?"

Nate bobbed his chin. "Yup. A bunch of folks in bandannas, carrying knives and such."

"All right, officers," Rocky snorted. "I can see the local busybodies have been sniffing around. I'm one of the bunch, as you put it. We like to hang out on the beach. What of it?"

"Who is in your, er, group?" Nate asked.

"Just me; my sister, Evelyn; and Dale Palmer, Rudy Anderson, and Dan Finch. They work the popcorn booth and run the jump house. Sometimes a few other festival roadies join in, but they're not here this time."

They stared at him in silence.

"We're friends, not felons. I'm sure you've checked. No arrests on my record."

"That's true. Maybe you just have really bad timing. Maybe you just happen to be around when tree farms burn and logging trails are blocked."

"And tree stumps are dumped," Nate added. "Don't forget the tree stumps."

Rocky threw the box down and kicked it into the corner. "I'm an ecologist. I'm interested in anything that threatens the natural balance of the earth. That doesn't make me a criminal."

"How about assault and battery? Does your group go in for that?"

"None of that, either."

"Were you on the beach last night?"

Rocky nodded. "Yeah. Some friends and I hiked up to the top of Finny's Nose. Then we stopped at the beach before we went back to our trailers for the night."

"What time, exactly?"

"We hit the beach about four o'clock, I'd say. But we didn't see another soul the entire time. We didn't see anybody, and we certainly didn't beat anyone up."

Jack tried to ignore his growling stomach. He wished he had made it through a few more of Bobby's pancakes before he was summoned to the beach. "I understand you have some difficulties with Bing Mitchell. You two have been mixing it up since you blew into town."

"My only difficulty with him is that he's a pig. Other than that, I got no problem with him." Rocky swiped at the crystal moon that hung from the tent. "Why? Was he the beaten-up guy?"

"No," Jack said.

"Too bad."

"Are you sure you don't want to tell us anything else? Like what does Bing have that your sister had to sell her car to pay for?" Jack decided it was the right moment to use the interesting tidbit that Ruth uncovered after the food fight.

Rocky's mouth opened and closed.

Jack remained silent, staring at him.

"Okay." Rocky looked at the ground. "The creep taped one of our protests. He got us doing something that might be considered questionable."

"Go on," Jack prodded.

"The stump thing. He videotaped us breaking into the city council offices with the stump."

Nate huffed into his mustache. "Definitely qualifies as questionable."

"I don't know how he found out about it, but he said if we didn't give him five thousand dollars, he would send the tape to the cops. I said go ahead, but my sister was upset. I couldn't let her get into any trouble, so I sold the car and paid the guy off."

"Did he give back the tape?"

He fixed them with a glare. "No, he did not. Now is there anything else you want? I've gotta get to work."

"Just one more thing. If, during your stay in Finny, you happen to trespass on Vern Rosario's property with or without spikes in your possession, you will be arrested."

Rocky's eyes widened, and his mouth gaped.

"We'll talk to the other people in your group to see if they have anything to add," Jack said.

"Go right ahead." Rocky took a step toward them. His eyes glittered behind the thick lenses. "Just see that you don't harass my sister."

Jack locked eyes with him. "We're not in the business of harassing people, Mr. Bippo." He zipped his denim jacket against the chill outside the booth. "You ought to be careful, though. That almost sounded like a threat."

19

September the 13th, 1923

The weather is miserable, cold. Just ripe enough for a nasty drizzle. We returned to the awful spot to pray. There we stood, under the great fir tree. It was so terribly lonely. Just this one blackened tree and no others to stand near. What we need is a good downpour to wash away the horrible stain of evil.

Janey has been completely incoherent since the fire. She just rocks back and forth in a daze. I wonder if she will survive the week. Dan came to see her, but she didn't seem to know who he was. He looked like a dead man, just enough life in him to pump his lungs, not enough to reach his broken heart. He wouldn't take a bite or even a drop of coffee to warm himself.

There is a terrible anger burning deep down in his eyes. I think he has in mind an act of vengeance. As much as I would like to see Slats punished for the terrible thing he did to that poor girl, I tremble to think of Dan going after that heartless monster on his own. I fear he will not live to enjoy his revenge.

Ruth finished reading the journal passage a minute before the doorbell rang. She turned the knob with a sweaty palm. She expected it to be Maude with a terse reminder that she was supposed to photograph the winner at the sand sculpture competition and closing ceremonies. Or maybe Flo coming by to pick up the brownies she'd made to include in a care package for Hugh.

Instead, Jack stood hand in hand with his son, Paul. He held out a bag of apples in greeting. "Hello. Maybe you'll know what to do with some of these apples. So far Boo Boo is the only one eating them, and I don't think dogs are supposed to have that much fiber."

"How nice," she said. "They sort of scream apple pie with big globs of ice cream to me." She knew perfectly well the fruit provided an excuse for the detective to check up on her, and she appreciated it.

"As long as I get a piece, I think that's an excellent idea."

"Come in. Hi, Paul. How are you doing today, little man?"

Paul nodded, looking around. "Cootchie?"

Ruth felt a pain stab through her like an electric shock. "I'm sorry, Paul. Cootchie has gone away for a while. We'll have to find things to do without her."

He toddled off toward the backyard, leaving Ruth and Jack alone.

She swallowed hard. "Jack, I know you wouldn't ever want to hurt my feelings. But really, I—I would understand if you—didn't want me to watch Paul next week."

He looked at her for a moment, his dark eyes warm. "I am perfectly comfortable that you will take excellent care of Paul as you always have. What happened up nose happened because of some sicko who, for whatever reason, wanted to scare all of us. It did not happen because you were negligent."

"Thank you." She tried to blink back tears as they followed Paul into the yard. When she could trust her voice again, she went on. "How is the investigation going? Both Cootchie's and Ed Honeysill's, I mean."

They watched as Paul stalked Grover, who danced out of the boy's path.

"Well, I gotta tell you. This is stretching our resources a bit. We haven't had one bit of info about the owner of the missing toe, and as for the kidnapper, all we've got is Cootchie's description of a man with glasses and a hat driving a pickup, or maybe a snowplow, depending on what she's been reading before we ask her."

Ruth laughed.

"As for the Honeysill case, plenty of people with the means to fire a flare gun and dump it in the grass at the edge of the parking area. No prints. No witnesses as everyone seemed to be looking up at the time. There were plenty of men wearing glasses of one type or another in the crowd. Plenty of strangers in town, even a loan shark from New York that we've got our eyes on. We don't figure he came into town for the fog."

"You know, Al at the bakery was telling me about a city type who came in. He said the man didn't exactly blend in with the surroundings."

"It's possible Honeysill got himself in some financial trouble and somebody was settling a score. Or maybe he wasn't the target. The killer might have assumed Bing was in the balloon. It seems a few people have it in for him, too."

"Do you think. . ." Her voiced trailed off.

"On the surface it doesn't seem like the murder and Cootchie's kidnapping were related," he said softly, "but we're going to check out every possibility."

She swallowed. "And now Hugh Lemmon is attacked. What is going on in this town?"

"I've been wondering that myself."

He walked over to the concrete bins. "I still think it's amazing that you can farm worms. Does that make you a wormologist?"

"A vermiculturist, actually." They both laughed. "I should tell you that I talked to Cootchie on the phone and she said the 'muffin man' took her."

He frowned. "What does that mean, exactly?"

"I don't know. The only Muffin Man I know is that character in the Mother Goose rhyme."

"Hmm. I'll run that by Nate. He's a master of all things Mother Goose. I've got to get going now. Louella is waiting for Paul, and in the middle of all this chaos, Bobby seems to think I need to go for a nature walk." His smile was eager, and she noticed a faint whisper of cologne.

She smiled back at the detective. "Okay. Thanks for coming by, and give my love to Bobby."

Jack collected Paul and left.

When they were gone, she plopped onto the sofa and breathed in the quiet.

Wait a minute. She sat up abruptly.

What had Jack said about the Honeysill investigation?

"Plenty of men wearing glasses of one type or another in the crowd."

And Cootchie's kidnapper wore glasses, too.

She felt suddenly sick to her stomach. It was possible that the person who murdered Ed Honeysill and the kidnapper were one and the same in spite of Jack's reassurance.

She shivered and went to lock the door.

The sand sculpture competition was set to commence at 11:00 a.m. after the tide went out and with plenty of time to wrap everything up before it returned. Ironically, the weather was once again magnificent with not a wisp of fog anywhere to be seen.

Most of the coastline that snuggled against the nostril portion of Finny's Nose was gravel strewn and rugged. Treacherous riptides had been known to snatch unsuspecting beachcombers from the sharp rocks where they delved for treasure. There was really only one stretch of beach suitable for a sand sculpture contest.

The gentle inlet had been known as Honey Beach since the early thirties when it was used to land boats carrying crates of sweet clover honey. On this day, Finny natives were working hard to take full advantage of the waning hours of the festival, and the tiny beach was crammed with people.

Ruth waved to Bubby, who stood next to a trailer that housed his boat, *The Stinky Limpet*. The Sassie sisters were haggling with him about the price of a charter fishing excursion. They gripped a set of fishing poles menacingly, both iron-gray heads wagged in unison. Judging by the disgruntled look on their faces, they had not fully recovered from losing the previous weekend's cooking contest to the salmon smokers. She hoped for Bubby's sake the day would not end in a mutinous uprising aboard his vessel.

Bobby stood with Monk behind a plywood table. Their sign boasted cold drinks, coffee, and homemade cookies. "Hey, Ruth," she called. "How come you aren't working behind the counter today?"

"I've got to attend to my photography duties. I did contribute a couple dozen cookies, however. Chocolate chip and oatmeal raisin."

"You did?" She lifted a layer of tinfoil from the top of a paper plate. "I only see oatmeal raisin."

Monk became suddenly busy counting out stacks of napkins and fiddling with the thermos of coffee.

"Uncle Monk?" Bobby said accusingly.

"Hmmm? Oh. Well, I thought they were for me." He reddened. "I love those chocolate chip pecan ones. It isn't fair to tempt me. It's like putting a rabbit in front of a greyhound."

The three of them laughed.

"I just saw Candace in front of the hotel," Bobby said. "She said they've given her the go-ahead to fly home for Ed's funeral."

"Oh." Ruth's thoughts flashed momentarily back to Phillip's funeral. Though she couldn't remember most of it, she hoped Candace would salvage some peace of mind by laying her own husband to rest.

Thinking about Candace's betrayal of her spouse, Ruth wondered if guilt would be a part of the woman's life for the rest of her days.

"It's a good thing the Fog Festival is about over," Monk said. "I don't think this town can handle much more drama."

"That reminds me. How is Hugh doing?" Bobby asked.

"Flo stopped by to see him, and she says he's doing well. Sore and bruised but nothing permanently damaged. He'll be back in action by the time we harvest the next set of mushrooms for Dimple." Saying her name gave Ruth a pang of sadness.

"And no arrests?" Bobby asked, pouring sugar packets into a bowl.

"Not that I've heard of."

Maude marched by with a roll of fluorescent pink string and a handful of wooden stakes.

"You looking for a vampire or something?" Monk called out.

"Funny," she said, glaring from under her fringe of bangs. "For your information, we have a last-minute entry to the contest. That makes twelve spots we've sold at ten dollars apiece."

"That's wonderful," said Ruth. "What's the winning prize?"

"A twenty-pound wheel of cheese."

"Cheese?"

"It's very good cheese," she said, her thimble of a nose pointed aloft. "Aged and extra sharp." She stalked off toward Bubby.

"Describes Maude to a tee." Monk chortled.

Ruth wished Monk and Bobby luck and went in search of the perfect Kodak moment.

True to her word, Maude had staked out twelve five-foot-square sections of beach for each contestant. Each square was filled with a collection of buckets, shovels, water bottles, and spatulas. A teenage boy was hard at work in one square sculpting a fighter plane. His face was fixed in concentration as he smoothed the wings with a Popsicle stick. Ruth took his picture, thinking he must be a real cheese lover to go to such lengths on a sunny Sunday morning.

The next contestant wore a fuzzy knit hat over his equally fuzzy hair. He was on hands and knees working a trowel over the perfect rectangle he had created.

"Hi, Alva. I didn't know you entered the sand sculpture contest."

The old man smiled broadly. "I want to win that cheese. Extra sharp and aged."

"So I've heard." She watched him for a few minutes as he fussed and fidgeted over the rectangle. As far as she could see, he was not making any attempt to transform the angular sand pile into anything recognizable. "What exactly—I mean, what type of sculpture are you working on?"

"Cancha tell?"

She peered at the rectangle again. "I give up. What is it?"

"It's a sandwich," he said with glee.

"Ahhh," she said. "Now I can see it. Good luck, Alva."

"Thanks, sweet cheeks."

She took his picture as she moved on.

There were a few other notable sculptures. Ruth was impressed with the mermaid rising from square number six. Her hair spread around her, and a giant tail curled above the sand. Many spectators shared words of encouragement with the sculptor.

Ellen towered over the men with arms crossed across her own much less impressive cleavage. "Ridiculous," she said as Ruth took a picture. "All this work for a wheel of cheese. They could have at least thrown in a magazine subscription or something."

Ruth left the librarian to her glowering and walked to the edge of ocean and sand. A woman stood several yards away, framed by the turbulent ocean.

Evelyn appeared to be watching the foaming scallops wash over her toes. She wore tomato-colored pants and a stained jacket. Her long hair whipped around in the breeze. A tiny dog was tucked under her arm.

"Hi, Evelyn. Did you come to see the sand sculptures?"

"Yes. Did you bring your birds?"

"Maude wanted me to being them as some sort of tourist attraction, but they don't get along well with the able-bodied of the species." She gestured to the mob of birds, wings outstretched, undulating around the children with food in their hands. "I see you've got a friend there."

She stroked the tiny dog carefully. "His name is Gulliver. He's eleven years old. Nobody wants a dog that old." Her voice was stained with sadness.

"Then I guess he's really lucky to have you."

Evelyn stared at her. "Sometimes," she said softly, "I feel as alone as they do."

The wind blew the hair away from her face, and Ruth could see the sadness nestled in her eyes. "I think everyone feels that way at one time or another."

"There doesn't seem to be a point to things anymore. I just move from one place to the next, but I don't feel like a part of any of it." She looked a Ruth with desperate eyes. "It feels more like existing than living. Have you ever felt like that?"

"Oh yes," Ruth said quietly. "I have felt exactly like that."

Evelyn opened her mouth then closed it, but the question remained on her face.

For a moment there was only the sound of the waves. Ruth felt a surge of courage in her heart. Before her brain had a chance to stifle it, she spoke. "There is Someone who can help you, who will be there to love you when the world lets you down. Someone who will never betray you."

They locked eyes for a moment. Ruth wondered if she had offended the woman. Evelyn stayed silent.

"If you ever want to talk, about Him, we can do that."

The tiny dog licked Evelyn's chin. "Thank you. Maybe—maybe we could talk, sometime."

"I would like that."

Evelyn gave Ruth a weary smile and left.

She watched Evelyn leave, each step etching a stamp in the sand. Ruth hoped fervently that those steps would lead her home.

Though her heart was light, her head was pounding when she made it back to her cottage. The strange home she had made with a flock of crippled birds and a pasture full of worms seemed pretty tame compared to the wild world outside. *Well,* she thought, *today is the last day of this awful festival. Maybe things will return to normal again.*

She thought about the toe and the murder and the terrifying disappearance of Cootchie Dent. The dark musings consumed her until she recalled the strange wondering look on the face of Evelyn Bippo. Suddenly a distant crack made her jump. Could it be a gunshot? No, probably a firecracker tossed by an errant festivalgoer. Jack would probably be more relieved than she when the Fog Festival staggered to a close. It would be heavenly to have things return to normal.

She thought of the growing closeness between Bobby and Jack.

Then again, maybe a few changes might be in order.

20

Jack couldn't see her from his position on his stomach behind a rock. Though it was irrational to blame all his trouble on the ridiculous festival, he couldn't wait for the event to be over. Things were not safe, he tried to explain to Bobby on the phone, and he didn't want her charging up Finny's Nose unescorted. She hadn't listened, of course.

Now, as he sheltered himself behind the rock pile, he prayed she wasn't going to pay a terrible price for her impatience. His heart refused to let him consider a tragic outcome. Not now, not Bobby.

The afternoon sun temporarily blinded him. He could hear the shots whacking into the dirt and trees just in front of him. He thrust his head above the granite edge, trying to get a shot off, but the sting of flying rock chips caused him to recoil. It would be another five minutes until backup arrived, even with Mary Dirisi at the wheel. Heart pounding, muscles tensed, he made a decision.

"We're going to have to do this the hard way." Scuttling on his belly around the outcropping, praying he wasn't stirring up any dust, he did a slow count to ten before he launched himself into the clearing and dove behind a twisted clump of trees.

Two shots zinged over his head, and then there was silence.

He crouched in as small a ball as he could manage and listened.

Nothing.

Ten seconds later he heard a small crack and the quiet crunch of leaves.

Creeping forward, both hands around the gun barrel, he poked his head around the pile of rock obscuring his sight.

"Hey there," she said, her voice weak. "I thought you decided to go for coffee." She was sitting hunched over, back against the rocks, blood dripping down the side of her face.

He took a steadying breath, noting the tightly controlled look of pain on her face. "No coffee. How badly are you hurt?"

"I'm not sure yet. How many of you are there?"

He swallowed. "Just one, I'm afraid."

"Hmmm. Then I think I may have some sort of head injury."

"Okay," he said, holstering his gun and feeling her arms and legs. "Any bullet holes I should know about?"

"No, and don't think this is going to get you out of going for a run with me," she said.

"Never crossed my mind." She winced as he passed a hand over her bloodied head. "Good thing you have excellent reflexes."

"Yeah. I felt the shot graze my hair and I dove. Unfortunately, I think I was a tad anxious and I rolled headfirst into a boulder. Who is shooting at us, by the way?"

He continued his examination, running fingers along the back of her neck. "I don't know, but we need to move. Are you up to it?"

"Sure."

He helped her up and then caught her as she collapsed again, vomiting on his shoes. He lowered her back to the ground, brushed the hair out of her eyes, and wiped her mouth with his shirtsleeve.

"I'm really sorry about that," she said.

"No problem. I've been through worse. Let's try it again, this time more slowly."

He raised her to her feet. She stood, clinging to his arm, her face pasty white.

"Okay?" he whispered.

She nodded.

"We're going to have to run for it, back to the trees. It's not far." He forced his voice to sound light, encouraging. He tried to ignore the quantity of blood staining her shirtfront and the glazed expression beginning to creep into her eyes. She was going into shock.

He counted softly to three, and then they ran, stumbling along to the tree line until he threw himself down on top of her, covering her head as best he could. Shots drilled into the trunks above, speckling them with splintered wood.

After a few minutes, the shooting stopped, replaced by the wail of sirens and running boots. Nathan hurled himself to the ground next to Jack, panting, eyes wide.

"You okay?" he asked.

"Yeah. She's hurt. Did you get him?"

"No. Mary and Yolo drove up the access road. Nothing yet. You think it's a single shooter?"

He nodded. "Reloaded twice. I think I heard him

running downhill."

Nate eyed the pale form between them. "Ambulance won't start. They're sending a rig up, but it won't do the slope very fast."

While they exchanged information, Jack rolled Bobby over, peeling the blood-soaked hair off her face.

She was still and drained of color.

"Where is the engine?" he shouted. "Never mind, we're taking her now."

He lifted the woman in his arms and carried her to Nate's squad car.

Her blood tattooed a trail on the slope of Finny's Nose.

He was on his fourth cup of coffee in the Eden Hospital waiting room when Ruth found him.

"Hi, Jack. How is Bobby doing?"

"She's going to be okay. She got a fairly good concussion, and she's been pretty out of it since we made it here. Doctor says she needs to stay quiet until tomorrow, and then they'll do another CAT scan."

She was glad to see only a shade of worry in his eyes. Monk had told her he was on the verge of panic when they met at the hospital earlier. "Any leads on the shooter?"

He grinned at her. "You're beginning to sound almost coplike, Ruth. Must be from your frequent brushes with the law. We don't have any leads yet, other than it was someone who knows the area real well. Lots of empty shell casings sent to the lab, but that's about it."

"Hmmm." Ruth nodded. "Would you mind telling me what Bobby was going to show you up nose? I saw her up there as I was on my way down from Pistol Bang's a few days ago, and she said she was doing homework so she could show you something. What was it?"

"Let's see—it kind of slipped my mind, what with everything that followed. She called me about two thirty or so and asked me to meet her at the top. What did she say?" His eyes searched the ceiling for an answer. "She said something about trees, fir trees, something weird about the cluster of trees at the top." He chuckled. "Frankly, I didn't really get where she was coming from, but that's not unusual for me when it concerns Bobby."

"You really like her, don't you?"

He looked down at his work boots. "Yeah. I really do."

"Well, when she wakes up, you tell her I'm bringing her an éclair. Her uncle has been busily baking batches of them for her. I know those things have mystical healing powers in addition to the five thousand calories and a bushel of fat."

"Excellent." Jack smiled at her. "What intriguing thoughts are going on in that head of yours? What's up with the tree thing?"

"I'm not sure. I was considering about taking a walk up nose before dark. Do you think it's safe?"

"We've still got people up there, so it's pretty quiet." He stretched and resettled himself in the chair. "Take Monk with you anyway."

21

"Why are we climbing up this infernal hill again?" Monk's cheeks were ruddy, and he was panting.

"I don't know exactly. It's just that Bobby was interested in something about the trees up here, and I just can't get it out of my mind. There is something up here that is the key to this whole mess." Ruth stopped as they crested the nose. "Let's sit down for a minute and cogitate."

He settled his large frame on a rock. "I'll give it a try, but my cogitator is low on fuel. Seeing Bobby hurt and all that just really took it out of me." He cleared his throat.

She joined him and patted his leg, saying another silent thank-you prayer for Bobby's safety. The late afternoon sun silhouetted an enormous Douglas fir against the sky. Ruth studied the tree standing sentinel over the younger trees nearby. She thought about Pickles Peckenpaugh's journal recounting the horrible tragedy that had taken place atop Finny's Nose. Could this be the very same tree? There was no outward sign of the crime; the charred bark would have grown over long ago in any case. Was it under these same boughs that the young girl Janey was found and later the body of Slats the gangster, who undoubtedly died at the hands of Soapy Dan?

Restlessly Ruth clambered down off the rock and walked under the spreading branches. The ground was damp and sticky, speckled with uneven patches where something, presumably squirrels, had been at work. Looking down from her vantage point, she counted four more fir trees, evenly spaced on each side of the parent. Standing where she imagined the women of the Pickle Jar had gathered, she could hear echoes of voices from decades past.

"There we stood, under the great fir tree. It was so terribly lonely. Just this one blackened tree and no others to stand near."

A lone fir. No others to stand near.

Yet as Ruth stood there in the gathering fog, she was yards away from four other fir trees. Younger trees, but still with many decades of growth to their credit. Perfectly spaced, equidistant from the giant fir.

Ruth looked down at the dark soil beneath her feet. Something looked familiar about the surface. The nubbly, tubular trails of earth that poked out here and there amid the rocks and needles.

Of course! Her worm castings. They were so plentiful around the base of the tree that she knew they had to have been placed there. Dug in here and there with a trowel or rake. Those had to be her castings. But why bring them up here? Why steal them at all for that matter?

She continued to walk under the scented branches, lost in thought, until she felt her foot sink into something soft and pliable. Looking down, she screamed.

Monk made it to her side with remarkable speed for a man of his bulk. "What is it? Are you hurt?" he yelled.

She could only point to the mass at her feet.

"Leaping lentils," he said, kneeling to examine the heap.

The squirrel's leg was trapped by the metal jaws. Its eyes were closed, breath coming in pants.

"Man. That's an awful way to catch something. These bear traps have been illegal forever. Alva said he found one this week and brought it to the police. What kind of an idiot would use a bear trap to catch a squirrel?"

"Good squirrels is dead squirrels," Ruth whispered, feeling the bile rise in her throat. "Can you free him?"

Monk didn't seem to hear her as he knelt closer. Carefully he wrapped a handkerchief around the squirrel's head to protect from getting bitten. With a supreme effort he managed to open the trap wide enough for her to remove the injured animal. "We'll take him up to the doc. She may be able to fix him up."

She took off her sweater and wrapped the poor shivering animal inside the soft folds. "You'll be okay. The doctor will take care of you." Turning to Monk, she asked, "Who would do such a terrible thing?"

He poked at the hinge with a stick. "Look at this. There's some white leather caught in here. Like the kind they make sneakers with. You don't suppose this trap caught more than a rodent, do you? Kinda brings to mind a certain toe we've got floating around Finny, don't you think? Ruth?"

She was staring into Monk's face, a look of horror frozen onto her own. "Monk. I know who the muffin man is."

He looked at her as though she were speaking in another language. "Huh?"

She felt a fierce tide of protectiveness swelling inside of her. The muffin man had taken her little family, the family she'd worked so hard to build, and brought it to the edge of disaster. Life had taken her first husband without so much as a warning. God had blessed her with another family, strange as it was, and she knew that it was in grave danger. A strength swirled inside her that she'd never felt before. In a blink, Ruth was suddenly concretely positive that no earthly being could be allowed to take Dimple and Cootchie away, too. She knew what she had to do. With God's help, it was time to make things right.

"Monk, we need to find Jack and Dimple right away."

22

Ruth read lots of mysteries. She knew how confronting a killer was supposed to work. Not that she expected to encounter the murderer at Dimple's farm. She'd frantically called everywhere looking for Dimple as they raced to town with no success. The phone at Pistol Bang's gave her an endless busy tone, which made her heart beat a panicked staccato.

Monk clicked off his cell phone, panting slightly. "Jack's just returning from a meeting. I left him a message to meet us up nose."

"We can't wait. We've got to get to Pistol Bang's and warn Dimple, if she's there. I just can't stand the thought that she might be in trouble."

"I've got your back, Ruth. Let's go."

It took them another twenty minutes to make it from the vet's office back to the top of Finny's Nose. The farm was quiet, without a sign of movement anywhere, until a noise from the polytunnel made them jump.

Monk lowered his voice to a whisper. "Probably just a squirrel on the roof, but I'm going to check it out. You stay here, Ruth."

She waited with her stomach in knots while Monk disappeared around the corner of the tunnel. Unable to remain still, she tiptoed to the office to peek in the window. A muffled noise made her whirl back in the direction of the tunnel. She heard Monk holler and bang against the door, which was now wedged with a piece of metal pipe.

She took a halting step to free her husband from his impromptu prison when she saw him.

Ruth recalled those satisfying literary conclusions in which the hero confronted the villain in the inevitable showdown, calmly laying out the facts in a careful, orderly fashion, while the police waited in the wings to apprehend him or her.

She reviewed these facts in her mind. Now that the moment had come and she was face-to-face with a killer, her mouth took an entirely different tact.

"What is the matter with you? Your father works hard for a living every day of his life, and you reward him by killing people? Why, Hugh?"

He looked at her calmly, hands tucked into the pockets of his corduroy pants. "I don't know what you're talking about."

"You jolly well do know what I'm talking about. I know you've been farming truffles at the top of Finny's Nose. I also know you killed Ed Honeysill and tried to kill Bobby Walker."

He sighed, wiping his nose on his sleeve. "I wouldn't expect you to understand. You're one of those complacent old-timers, content to live out your days on social security benefits until you die. You think too small to come up with a way out." There was a sullen glint in his prominent eyes behind the glasses.

"Ah yes, the brilliant plan. The plan where you inoculate the trees at the top of Finny's Nose with truffle spores and grow them yourself, selling them as French exports at triple your cost. Never mind that the land doesn't belong to you, you idiot."

"Who cares who it belongs to? Nobody uses it anyway."

"I see. So you cooked up the idea to farm the truffles. You transplanted new trees, I noticed. When, exactly, will the younger ones start producing truffles?"

"I don't know for sure. I moved them from another part of the nose. They're about fifteen years old, but I've already harvested some smaller truffles. It's all experimental. In five years or so, I will have some grade-A truffles. Until then, I have the crop from the mature tree. Soon I'll have enough socked away to go wherever I want to."

"When did you become a truffle expert?"

"While the others were out at dances and parties, I was working. I've always been working, since I was a kid. My high school agriculture class gave me the basic tools to learn about inoculation and hybridization. When my blue geranium project went up in smoke, I began working on introducing spores to the root system of host trees. It's not hard; it just takes patience. You just have to manage the pests, especially the squirrels. And then there are the human pests." Hugh spat out the words, shifting his weight off of his left leg.

Ruth's mind flashed to the toe. "That was your toe; you cut off your own toe with the bear trap, didn't you? Was that part of the plan?" Somehow the antagonistic tone of her voice did not fit with her literary image of the cool detective, but she could not stop the anger that was humming in her veins. A pain began to throb in her temples.

"I was trapping the vermin, and I stepped in my own

trap," he replied, shifting his weight again. "While I was tying up my foot, a Steller's jay took off with the toe." A drop of spittle flew from his mouth.

Ruth suppressed a rift of laughter.

"That's the only thing that went wrong, anyway. My next crop is ready to harvest, and I have buyers all lined up. Then I can pay off the money I owe and it's all profit."

"What money?"

"I had to borrow some money for the spores, the Web site, a new truck, that kind of thing. My father certainly wouldn't cough up a penny to help me."

"Who loaned you the money?"

"Some people." He looked sullen.

A light flashed in her mind. "Oh, I get it. You borrowed money from a loan shark. Jack mentioned there was one in town." She thought back to the day Alva found Hugh on the beach. "So that's who beat you up and left you on the beach—not the bandanna gang."

"The truffles weren't ready as soon as I thought they would be. I couldn't pay off the loan on time." Hugh shook his head. "I tried to tell them I would have the money soon, but they wouldn't listen. That's the problem today." His voice rose in volume with each word. "No one listens!"

"Gee," she said, ignoring his raging, "crooks with no patience. Imagine. That's when you decided to blame your beating on Rocky and his group?"

"I saw them on the beach a couple of times, and they kept poking around my trees up nose. I figured accusing them would explain things. They're crazy anyway. I set fire to one guy's trailer to keep him from sniffing around near my truffles." He ran rigid fingers through his hair. "It's okay. It's all okay. My plan is working out in spite of everything."

Suddenly his face changed. The last trace of youthful enthusiasm melted away, leaving something crazed in its wake.

Ruth should have been terrified, but the fear did not succeed in uprooting the anger that vibrated in her gut. "So you don't figure murdering Ed was a tiny snafu in your plan? Why did you have to kill him?"

"Ed was suspicious; he knew my truffles weren't French. He kept pressuring me to see them, sample them. I saw him and the dark-haired girl up looking at my trees. He left a message at Dimple's asking to see me before he left town. I knew he figured it out, so I had to get rid of him."

Hugh's prominent Adam's apple bobbed up and down as he spoke. "I didn't really think he would die when I shot the balloon down. I thought he would get scared and go home. Then that girl came sniffing around, measuring the trees and examining the ground underneath. She was close to figuring out they were transplanted or seeing evidence of my cultivation. I should have killed her, too, but I'm not a good shot." The words tumbled out faster and faster, like cockroaches after filth.

She knew she should feel sorry for this young man. His mind had been fractured beyond repair. But her heart could not pity the man who had taken Cootchie away.

"Look on the bright side," she spat, "at least you didn't shoot off your other toe. And then the best part of your plan. You decided to kidnap Cootchie. That's right, isn't it? You were the man with the glasses who took her, weren't you?" The words snapped out of her mouth.

"Yeah, no big thing. I wore a wig and a fake mustache. She didn't even recognize me. I took her to Half Moon Bay and left her at the library. It got you all out of my hair for a while," he said, rooting around in his pocket. "It got all the festival nuts off my land while everyone looked for Cootchie, especially those tree freaks. They kept trampling my truffles." He sniffed. "I didn't think it would be such a big deal anyway. I wouldn't have done it if I had known Dimple would be so upset."

Ruth thought about Cootchie's phone conversation. It wasn't the muffin man she referred to, but the truffle man. The man she had seen at the park when he spilled the truffles on the ground. "She's smarter than you think, Hugh. As a matter of fact, I think she's smarter than you, period."

A deep flush mottled his cheeks. "That's where you're wrong. Where everyone has always been wrong. I'm not just a geek, some loser farm boy. You go ahead and laugh, but I'll have the last laugh in the end."

His eyes glittered in the afternoon sun. "Besides, how is this your business anyway? You didn't even know Ed, and Bobby Walker is fine. So I took Cootchie for a few hours. What's it to you? I didn't hurt her. There was no harm done."

Ruth felt as if his words came from far away. There was a rushing in her ears, and her temples pounded. She felt warm all over, as if her veins flowed with molten lava. "No harm done?"

By the time his hand emerged from his pocket with the switchblade, she had grabbed the log that stood upright near her feet. She did not feel the knife slice into her forearm as she swung the log like a baseball bat, smashing it down onto his injured foot.

He doubled over in pain but quickly straightened again and lunged with the knife. She swung again.

The log whacked into the side of his head with a satisfying thud and sent him crashing to his knees on the gravel path.

Not bad for someone who hasn't played baseball since the third grade, she thought. She hooked her hands under his armpits and dragged him to the sturdy oak post supporting the sign reading PISTOL BANG MUSHROOM FARM.

As she looked around, she spied the metallic cylinders. Smiling, Ruth Budge set to work.

Nine minutes later the detective was running up Pistol Bang's gravel walkway, gun drawn, with Nathan and Mary at his heels. Jack stopped short, almost causing his officers to plow into him from behind. Ruth sat on a wooden bench, tying up her bloody arm with the sleeve of her jacket.

Jack had to do a double take to realize that the

silver cocoon under the signpost was Hugh Lemmon wrapped from waist to crown of head in multiple rolls of duct tape. The only spots showing on his upper body were two dazed-looking eyes and his prodigious nose. The rest of him was completely mummified in silver tape.

Nate succeeded in freeing Monk from the tunnel.

Monk puffed up, gasping and red faced.

"Ruth, are you all right?"

"Yes, I'm fine. He only cut my arm, and I have a tremendous headache, but that's about all the damage. To me anyway," she said, continuing to wrap her arm.

"Ambulance is on—" Nate stopped talking as he got a good look at Hugh. "Er, ambulance is on its way. Does he need, uh, medical attention?"

"Oh, he may have a concussion or something. I hit him with a log. Other than that, I think he's just fine." She smiled. "Until they have to remove the duct tape, that is."

All three officers grinned.

Mary listened to a message on the radio. "Dimple is fine. She was off picking lentils or nettles or something."

With a deep sigh, Ruth stood up and brushed off her hands before she collapsed.

23

Ruth was staring at her IV, wondering if she could request a chocolate flavor, when the door opened.

"Hello, Ruth," Dimple said. Her green eyes were puffy with fatigue. "How are you?"

"I'm okay. I had to have a few stitches, and apparently the doctor decided to have my oil changed and air filter replaced while he was at it."

"That sounds practical."

"I'll probably go home this afternoon when the test results are in." The silence dragged on. "How is Cootchie?"

"She is having a lovely time with, uh, Meg. She said it's fun to play in the yard and look for bones. I think she might be disrupting Meg's landscaping, though."

The silence stretched into the uncomfortable zone.

"Dimple, I am so sorry. For letting him take Cootchie." She choked out the words.

Dimple laid her tiny hand on Ruth's arm. "Ruth, dear, you did not know the evil around you. Neither did I." She blinked back tears. "He was with me all the time. I trusted him. I trusted him around my daughter."

"If it means anything, I really don't think he meant to kill anyone. He just didn't see the reality of it. It was like something out of a movie."

Dimple looked away from Ruth. A phone buzzed somewhere in a distant corridor.

"What is it?" Ruth asked. "Tell me."

She took a steadying breath. "I'm going away for a while. I'll close the farm for a few months and go to stay with Meg in Arizona."

"I thought you might." An iron weight settled over her heart. "I can understand that, after everything that has happened."

"I won't stay. Cootchie and I will come back. I just want to know what it's like. To have a mother."

She nodded. "I will miss you so much."

"I will miss you, too." Dimple's long hair tickled Ruth's cheek as she leaned over to hug her. "The heart will always find the path towards home."

Ruth wondered despairingly if the path would end in Arizona with Meg.

Dr. Ing strode quietly into Ruth's hospital room a few hours later. As she listened to his words, she recalled his quiet, soothing tones years earlier when he explained how her husband of twenty-five years had suddenly stopped living. He was just as quiet and soothing now.

"Ruth, I have some news for you. We've run tests, as you know. I always like to do that as a precaution in cases like this."

Tests? Her heart beat faster.

"As much as we know about the human body, it's still a mysterious, enigmatic thing. People who should be dead live on for years. Perfect babies die without explanation."

She stared at him with wild fear that filled every pore.

He returned her gaze with eyes full of compassion. "I am afraid this is going to be a shock to you, Ruth, but I have no doubt that you will be able to handle it."

Monk rushed into the shop. Ruth was seated at a scarred wooden table an hour before her morning coffee shift would start. She stared out the window at the hydrangeas wearing their cotton-candy colors. She didn't meet Monk's gaze. He sat down next to her, removing the ever-present ladle from his pocket and squeezing the smooth metal handle.

"Honey, I've been so worried," he began. "I tried to find you, but you'd already gone." He paused, tapping his ladle on the table. "I wanted to take you home. They said you insisted on being discharged. Are you sure that was a good idea?"

"It was what the doctor told me," she mumbled as she continued to stare out the window. "They did tests, you know."

His breath hissed through his lips. "So the doctor did. . .tests?" He inhaled again. "I understand if you don't want to talk about it." He chewed his lower lip. "Maybe it's better to wrangle with it for a while, until you figure out how to deal with it, or treat it, or whatever." He paused again.

She turned to him. "I'll be forty-eight soon. That's

a long time to live, don't you think?"

Monk's eyes widened. "Yes, I guess so."

"I've lost a husband and become Nana to a stranger's child. I've even learned how to raise worms for a living and found another good man to love. Don't you think that's a full life?" She looked intensely at him now.

"Yes." He swallowed. "But whatever it is, it doesn't mean the end. We can fight it, or figure out how to live with it. People survive things all the time." His words tumbled out like tiny fish darting from a predator.

"That's what Dr. Ing said," Ruth said, her voice flat.

"I'll help you," he said. "We'll do it together. I will be here for you." His eyes were warm and filled with tears, radiating a tenderness that was at odds with his hulking stature and quick temper.

"I don't want to be a medical curiosity," she said, "some freak of nature."

He stood and put a huge hand on her shoulder. "Just tell me what to do, Ruth, how to help you. I'll do whatever I can."

"I know—" She suddenly realized that Monk thought she was dying of some disease.

What a precious man she'd married. She looked into his weathered face, reading the emotion flashing in his eyes. He had been there through it all. Steady and quiet. Ready to be asked about whatever she needed. She remembered his earlier words. God gave her strength because He wanted her to use it. She sat up straighter in the chair.

"Monk, it's not what you think. The doctor said I'm pregnant."

He jerked upward; the ladle flew out of his hand

and shattered the window into millions of sparkling droplets.

The crash reverberated all the way to the top of Finny's Nose.

Dana Mentink lives in California with her husband and two children. Her first love is the classroom; she has taught children from preschool through fifth grade for over a decade.

Dana is perpetually in search of a great story, either through painfully expensive trips to the bookstore or via her own labors in front of the computer. She enjoys writing cozies for Heartsong Presents—MYSTERIES! as well as suspense stories.

In addition to her novels, Dana writes short articles, both fiction and nonfiction, for a wide variety of magazines. Dana enjoys mentoring other writers and finding new vehicles to provide her readers with a hefty dose of mystery, merriment, and make-believe. Contact Dana on her Web site: www.danamentink.com

You may correspond with this author by writing:
Dana Mentink
Author Relations
PO Box 721
Uhrichsville, OH 44683

A Letter to Our Readers

Dear Reader:

In order to help us satisfy your quest for more great mystery stories, we would appreciate it if you would take a few minutes to respond to the following questions. We welcome your comments and read each form and letter we receive. When completed, please return to:

Fiction Editor
Heartsong Presents—MYSTERIES!
PO Box 721
Uhrichsville, Ohio 44683

Did you enjoy reading *Fog Over Finny's Nose* by Dana Metink?

Very much! I would like to see more books like this! The one thing I particularly enjoyed about this story was:

_____

_____

_____

Moderately. I would have enjoyed it more if:

_____

_____

_____

Are you a member of the HP—MYSTERIES! Book Club?
Yes ☐ No

If no, where did you purchase this book?

_____

Please rate the following elements using a scale of 1 (poor) to 10 (superior):

___ Main character/sleuth   ___ Romance elements

___ Inspirational theme   ___ Secondary characters

___ Setting   ___ Mystery plot

How would you rate the cover design on a scale of 1 (poor) to 5 (superior)? _____

What themes/settings would you like to see in future **Heartsong Presents—MYSTERIES!** selections? _____
_____
_____
_____

Please check your age range:

    ◌ Under 18   ◌ 18–24
    ◌ 25–34   ◌ 35–45
    ◌ 46–55   ◌ Over 55

Name: _____

Occupation: _____

Address: _____

E-mail address: _____